Four years ago, things had been very different. In trouble with the mob and suicidal, Aaron's twin brother, Troy, needed to get rid of his life. So he'd handed it over to Aaron. And when Aaron's impersonation of his twin brother was revealed, Aaron feared losing the man he loved, his brother Troy's husband, gorgeous personal trainer, David Alvarez. But by some miracle, David had fallen in love with Aaron, realizing that Aaron was good and true, the contrast to his twin, and there was forgiveness. When Troy's insane plot to let his twin take the fall of his screwed-up life unraveled and it appeared Troy's life was over, Aaron had hope that his life with David could truly begin.

Aaron and David now run a B & B on a beautiful Hawaiian island and life is great until the handsome and charming Randy Carlton buys the house down the beach from them. From the onset, Randy Carlton gives Aaron the feeling that he wants David. And he does.

Randy Carlton has gone to great lengths to get back what he considers to be his. He intends to let nothing stand in his way. He will have David at all costs . . . even if he has to kill to do it.

This book was previously published under the title Man in the Mirror: Mirrors, Book 2.

Man in the Mirror
Copyright © 2020 AJ Llewellyn and DJ Manly
ISBN: 978-1-4874-2913-3
Cover art by Martine Jardin

Published by eXtasy Books Inc or
Devine Destinies, an imprint of eXtasy Books Inc

Look for us online at:
www.eXtasybooks.com or www.devinedestinies.com

MAN IN THE MIRROR
MIRROR IMAGE BOOK 2

BY

AJ LLEWELLYN AND DJ MANLY

DEDICATION

To the memory of Michael Jackson . . . a true god of music . . .

*We look into mirrors but we only see the effects of our
times on us — not our effects on others.*
— Pearl Bailey

CHAPTER ONE

Gregory was seriously getting on his nerves today, but he could handle it. Soon enough, he'd be rid of him permanently, but there was one last thing to be done first. The only reason he'd lasted this long was because the guy had connections and the hefty inheritance he'd gotten from his oil rich granddaddy in Texas didn't hurt either. It had paid all his medical bills and given him a new lease on life. He hadn't touched a cent of the cash he'd stashed away. Now, he was just waiting for the money to clear from the house sale and he could move on to the last stage.

He watched Gregory through the mirror for a second. The dork was lying on the bed, playing with his cock just the way he'd ordered him to. He had on his thick, studded collar with a chain attached to the bed post. "Come on, Greg. Stroke it," he encouraged. "Stroke it good." If the guy wore himself out then he wouldn't have to fuck him later. *Please, pass out, you hairy son-of-a-bitch.*

Gregory was really slapping it hard now as he turned his attention to checking out his new black leather pants. He posed, puffing out his muscles as Gregory's chain knocked against the bed post. Working out had really paid off and you had to love the square jaw, high cheek bones, and full lips. The hair . . . all nicely streaked with blond highlights was so LA.

"You're beautiful," Gregory cried out. "I'm coming . . . ah, damn it . . . babe. Just looking at you . . . come over there and give it to me."

1

"Oh, sorry." He turned and shook his head. "You don't need me. You've done it on your own."

"I'll always need you. If it wasn't for you, I'd never have discovered the pleasures that I . . ."

"Yeah, yeah." He gave Gregory a tight smile. "It's true. You owe me. Now, finish up and . . . ah . . . change the sheets, will you? This room needs dusting as well." He walked over and undid the collar from the bedpost then left Gregory's room. He unlocked his own room, the room he kept all for himself, the place he shared with his own true love. He locked the door behind him, undid his leather pants, and pulled them off. He jumped onto the bed and took his cock in his hand. He stroked it slowly, his tongue moving around his lips then looked up at the full-blown photograph of the naked man he'd taped to the ceiling.

"Hi, baby," he said softly, stroking a little rougher. "Yeah . . ."

He breathed heavy. "I've missed you. So hot . . . gawd . . . um . . . yeah . . . fuck me. Fuck me, baby. A real man to take control, I miss you so much." He reached over for the dildo he kept on his night stand. He opened his legs and began to slowly penetrate himself with it. "It won't be long, my love. We'll be together again."

He pushed the instrument deeper then pulled out, gasping, his gaze fixed to the image. "Baby!" He cried out, his chest heaving. He fucked himself faster, harder. "He-has-my-life, my husband. He-ah . . . yeah . . . time-to-get-it . . . back!" He was coming, his body going into a spasm as he licked his lips and remembered . . . Dave . . . Dave . . . Dave!

He lay there in the aftermath of orgasm, his chest heaving. He turned his head and smiled, imaging Dave was there smiling back at him, hearing the words Dave was saying to him in his head. *"How was it, baby?"*

"Fantastic. But, Dave, my love," he said softly, "I've been

2

so bad. Such a bad boy. Are you going to punish me?"

"Oh yeah. I'll punish you. I'll spank you then fuck you until you pass out. I'll tie you up. Would you like that?"

"Oh yeah." He began to stroke himself again. "I'm sad. Only that naked picture I keep of you makes me happy. It was on our honeymoon, remember? What a stud you were . . . and I had that picture blown up. Shit, Dave. I can almost taste you."

"Don't be sad, my love. You know it's you I love. Only you."

"Then we have to get rid of him. Technically, you're committing adultery."

"Of course we'll get rid of him. Then we can be together. I was devastated when I thought you were dead. You realize a man like me has needs."

"But, baby, I know you have needs, raging . . . lusty needs, and I mean to fulfil all of them soon. Every last one."

"You're brilliant, baby. The way you seduced that pussy of a cop . . . and how another man . . . Hill's partner . . . was buried in your place. I'm a little jealous about how you made Gregory your slave. I don't like him touching you or you touching him."

"No, don't." He sat up in bed. He picked up the pillow and brought it to his lips. He kissed it, feeling as if his lips were on Dave's. He slid his hand down the pillow and clutched the material. "Um, your cock is hard for me again, Dave."

"Always hard for you."

"You used to wake up that way. God, I loved sucking your cock. I'm so sorry. I never meant to cheat on you. Please forgive me. I'm yours forever. Gregory means nothing to me, baby. You know that. He's a means to an end, that's all. And as soon as I'm done with him . . . he'll join his partner in the ground. You and I . . . Dave" — he hugged the pillow close — "we'll share the money, go anywhere you want, as long as you fuck me long and hard, as long as you make me your slave in bed . . . master me . . . master me like only you can, my beautiful lover . . . then . . . we get rid of my piece of trash brother in your bed." His lips curled into a sneer.

"That talk turns me on. I'm so hard. Tell me how you'll do it . . . how you'll get rid of him for good while I fuck you all night. Get on your knees. Get on your knees, you whore. Your ass is mine!"

He got down on the floor and closed his eyes. He imagined the weight of his love on top of his back, the penetration . . . Dave's cock splitting him wide . . . pumping him until he was flat on the floor. Dave, his Dave, with his beautiful body, incredible cock, was screaming his name.

"Troy! Troy!"

With his hand on his own cock, he came again and collapsed face down. He sighed, his eyes closing, Dave's face floating in front of him.

He fell asleep for a while. When he opened his eyes, it was dark. He left his room, locked the door behind him. He stood at the living room window waiting for Gregory to return. It was the man's last night on the LAPD. His last night for a lot of things. So nice. They'd transferred Greg to Hawaii. So lovely the weather there, especially in Kauai, on the North Shore. Troy just loved the beach, and Wainiha seemed perfect. Unspoiled paradise. The realtor had been a little surprised how swiftly Troy wanted to complete the sale. She kept trying to introduce the subject of fee simple versus leasehold, but Troy knew fee simple would appeal to the distressed homeowners. He would pay an extra chunk of money to buy the land beneath the house, apparently not a customary thing in Hawaii. It was fast becoming the way real estate agents and sellers could make an extra profit.

His cash purchase also eased the sellers' qualms about a loan application not being able to qualify with Hawaii's new, severe restrictions, owing to so many island foreclosures. The sellers agreed to everything, even immediate occupancy in exchange for cold, hard cash. This had the added benefit of no close scrutiny from anyone. Not the sellers' bank or the county assessor's office. The house would be his. He couldn't wait to get there.

When the headlights of Gregory's car shone in the driveway, Troy switched on a lamp. He sat down on the sofa and waited for the door to open. Gregory's house had been up for sale since Troy had made him put in for the transfer. Finally it was sold. They were supposed to find out from the bank today if the check had cleared. Troy needed that money. There was no way in hell he was going to touch the nest-egg he had put aside for Dave and him.

"Well?" he demanded, as Gregory came through the door. What an unlikely couple they presented, Gregory all gruff and ugly and he . . . beautiful . . . young . . . brand new. He couldn't wait to be rid of the man.

"The money is in my account," he said, taking off his gun holster.

Troy held out his hand. "Give me that. You know I don't like you carrying the gun in the house. Leave it in the car next time. Just take out the bullets."

"Sorry, baby," he murmured.

"So," Troy gave him a smile. "I'll come with you tomorrow. I have some expenses. We'll transfer it into my account."

"The bank will have already deposited the funds in mine and —"

"Then it won't be a problem to change it to mine." Troy put the gun in the drawer. "So, how was your last day?"

"A little sad to leave everyone at the station."

"Don't tell me you're having second thoughts?" Troy demanded. "I mean, if you want to break up with me . . ." He looked down, forcing the tears to come into his eyes.

"No, no, of course not." Gregory rushed over and sat beside him, hugging him. "Troy, I . . ."

"What did you call me?" His head shot up and he pushed him away. "Damn it, Gregory, you know I don't go by Troy. Shit!"

5

"I'm sorry, I mean . . . Randy. Such a beautiful name . . . and . . ."

"Yes, so . . . it's okay, babe . . . just don't forget it, okay?" *What a moron!*

"Can I call you Troy in bed?" he teased with a smile.

"No," Troy told him. "Not even there. Troy is dead, remember? I'm Randy Carlton now, and on the road to a successful modeling and film career."

"Yes, baby, and you're going to be big. Real big. A star. You have the body and the looks for it."

"Of course . . . and that brings me to . . . well . . . another topic." Troy sat back on the sofa. He took Gregory's hand. "We need to leave tomorrow, after the bank transfer."

"Tomorrow? I haven't even packed anything."

"Well, get to it, honey. The realtor is waiting for me to sign the papers for our new house. That's why I need the money in my account."

"I'm not sure about Hawaii, pet. I think your career would have a better chance here . . . or in New York even."

Troy shook his head. There was no point in telling poor Gregory that he would never see Hawaii. That would ruin everything. "I think my agent and I know more about that than you do."

"I suppose but . . . Troy, baby." He sighed. "I thought we'd get married first and —"

Troy jumped to his feet. "Damn it . . . you fucking asshole . . . I'm Randy. Randy!" He went to strike him then held back. He couldn't ruin it. He was so close. "I'm sorry." He shook his head. "Just listen to me, baby. I'm doing all this for us." He went to his knees and placed his head on Gregory's lap. Gregory reached out to touch his hair.

"I love you so much." Troy kissed his hand. He looked up at him. "I have an agent in Hawaii now. She says my future is there, and we have to play down our relationship a little. I need to give the appearance of being single . . . and straight, for a bit. We'll talk marriage later." *Besides, I have a husband, fool, and you couldn't shine a light on him.*

Gregory moaned. "Randy . . . please, I thought we'd stay in LA awhile. You promised we'd get married. I'd like to invite my friends."

"Shush, darling." Troy placed a finger on his lips. "You'll be my whore a while longer, okay?"

"Whore? Yeah, okay."

Troy smiled. That excited the poor sap. "Um, slut boy, whore, whipping boy, now, I'm going to take you to bed and use the whip on you tonight. Would you like that, sweet meat, my sweet, sugar honey?"

He nodded. "Talk dirty like that to me." His breath came fast.

"I will, and tomorrow, after we go to the bank, we'll rent a room at that little out-of-the-way hotel where I held you hostage, remember?"

"That place makes me so hard. It's where . . . you helped me know myself . . . appreciate pain and submissive devotion—"

Oh enough! "I know, baby. You came alive as my hostage . . . my sex toy. Listen, I'm going to give you the ultimate treat tomorrow . . . an orgasm you'll never feel again in your life. It will be just like . . . death."

Gregory squirmed a little on the sofa. He licked his lips and nodded. "Oh, that rundown hotel makes me feel like your bitch. Like old times."

"Like old times, what?" Troy demanded, getting to his feet.

"Master. Like old times, master."

"Say it like you mean it!" He slapped him in the face. "I'll hurt you."

"Yes, master, sir." He dropped to his knees and kissed his feet.

"There's a good boy." Troy stroked his hair. "Now, come on, slut. Time for your spanking." It was unfortunate. As annoying as Gregory was at times, he'd been indispensable. However, everything gets old and becomes no longer useful. He couldn't drag Gregory to Hawaii. He would be recognized and that wouldn't do. It wouldn't do at all.

The next day, Troy drove Gregory to the bank. "Now, let's deposit the funds into my account," Troy told him, "so I can pay for our new house in Hawaii."

"How much of it do you need?" Gregory eyed him.

"You know you're no good with money, sweetheart. Keep some pocket money, a few thousand, and transfer the rest to me. I'll take care of everything like I always do. You want things to be nice for us, don't you?"

Gregory nodded. Troy handed Gregory a pre-filled banking deposit slip and waited in the car. A half hour later, he came out and handed Troy the receipt. Troy checked the figures and smiled, leaning over to kiss him. "Perfect. It's all there. Now, your reward, love."

On the way to the hotel, Gregory asked Troy why he was wearing driving gloves. Troy grinned at him. "I'm getting into character for later." He winked. "It's a surprise."

"Okay," Gregory said, but then he started to whine about his furniture. "I still say we should have had the furniture transferred to our new place rather than let it go with the house. That dinette set was an antique. My grandmother left it to me and . . ."

"Gregory, don't ruin it for me. Stop crying over junk. We'll get new stuff."

"You were in such a hurry today. I didn't even get all my clothes."

"I'm sure the new owner will send you any junk you left behind. Now," Troy snapped, "do you want to go to our spot or not?"

Gregory mellowed. "Of course I do, baby."

Troy stopped at a red light, leaned over and kissed him. A little while later, he pulled the car to a stop across the street. "Listen, for fun, while I look for parking, you check in under an assumed name, let's say, Danny Pain, get it? Pay in cash."

"Okay." He laughed. "Danny Pain. Why?"

"Fantasy, just for fun, sweetie, get into it. It's sexy. Now, I'm going to call the hotel and ask for your room under that name. I have a surprise for you, something to get you going . . . I'm going to dress up. I'll have to sneak in so no one sees me in my get up. Answer as soon as I knock, okay?"

Gregory was breathing hard. "Okay, going now."

Troy took the car around the corner. He found a house that looked like no one was home and parked Gregory's car in their driveway. He hurried down the street toward the hotel with his small overnight bag. At the pay phone across the street from the hotel, he took off one of the gloves to dial the front desk and asked for the room of Danny Pain.

Gregory answered right away. "Hey, I'm ready. Come on up."

"Good. Can't wait. What room?"

"I asked for one on the second floor, room two-twelve. Baby, it's *the* room, the one at the end of the hall where we fell in love."

"Ah . . . how romantic." Troy rolled his eyes. "I'll be right there." Troy hung up and ran across to the hotel. With his head down, he waited until two men walked into the hotel lobby and up to the desk. The clerk was occupied with them so Troy took his opportunity and slipped inside the entrance. Quickly, he sprinted to the steps and ran up to the second floor.

Troy took out his leather mask and slipped it over his head. He knocked softly at the door of two-twelve, glancing around to make sure no one was coming down the hall.

Gregory answered the door. Troy pushed his way inside and shut the door, locking it behind him. He looked around. What a dump! No improvement since the last time he'd stayed here—all the same, right down to the threadbare curtains and stained sheets.

"What in hell are you doing still dressed?" he barked, walking over and bringing the curtains together. "Get your fuckin' clothes off now, you slut!"

Gregory quickly began to undress. Troy opened his bag. He took out a ball gag, handcuffs, cock ring, nipple clamps, and a scarf. He tossed them on the bed, one by one. He could see Gregory tremble in anticipation, as he checked out each article.

"Get on your knees on the bed!" he demanded.

Gregory did as he was told, all part of the games they played together. His cock was hard. Troy slapped it a few times. "I didn't tell you to get erect."

"Sorry, master." He winced. "Aren't you going to strip?"

"No. And don't tell me what to do. I give the orders." Troy grabbed Gregory's cock and wrapped the strap around it. Then he gripped his arms roughly and forced them behind his back, snapping on the handcuffs.

Gregory almost fell forward on his face.

Troy pulled him upright and slapped his face hard. "Stay still, fool!" He rolled his nipples between his fingers and clamped one then the other.

"Please," Gregory begged, licking his lips. "Ouch. They hurt."

"Good." It had to look real. He stood back and smiled then went back to his bag and found the studded collar. He'd put that on later. He lifted the chains from the clamps to Gregory's mouth. "Bite them. Pull up and feel the burn, baby."

"Um, so good." Gregory closed his eyes, yanking a little on the chains in his mouth.

"Now, spit them out. I got a nice ball gag for you . . . and how 'bout I grease up a nice fat dildo for your ass? Ask nicely."

"Please, master?"

"Say it."

"I want a big, fat cock in my ass."

"Um. Good." He smiled, dangling the ball gag. "Open wide, slut."

After securing the gag, Troy stroked his hair a few moments. He took his time greasing the dildo, running it across Gregory's chest, touching his swollen cock with it, his nipples. "Lift up for Daddy," he ordered and placed the oily sex toy under him. "Sit on it, you whore. Pansy, pussy! Let your ass eat it, cop."

Gregory bore down on the toy. A muffled moan came from his throat.

"You know," Troy told him, picking up the expensive silk scarf someone had bought him years ago, "I've fantasized about being in your place so many times. Don't you think, Gregory," he leaned in, his face close to his. "I'd like a real man once in a while, someone who could make me their slut for a change . . . I had that . . . you see . . . had a man that could make me beg . . . my husband." He showed him the scarf, pulling it taut in front of Gregory's startled eyes. "He's big and muscular . . . with a cock so sublime . . . I could come just looking at him . . . you'll never do that for me. So . . . unfortunately . . ."

He swung the scarf in behind Gregory's neck and pulled from side to side as he spoke. "You can't go with me to Hawaii because I'm going there to get back what belongs to me . . . Dave. My beautiful, hot David . . . and see . . ." He grinned. "You can't come because he'd recognize you, him and that whore of a brother of mine." Troy crossed the scarf in the front of Gregory's throat and tied it tight. Then, he whipped off the cock ring and began to jerk him off. "I promised you death . . . so . . ." He gritted his teeth, grabbing both ends of the scarf together and pulling tighter while he continued to stroke him for a few seconds then backed away. He watched as the life slowly went out of Gregory's eyes and he flopped forward onto the bed.

Troy pulled his hand away from Gregory's cock, wiping it on the sheet. He left the scarf tied at the neck then pushed Gregory's head back up to attach the studded collar. "Terrible accident," he said softly, shaking his head. "Such a scandal too . . . a detective . . . who knew that cops were into this stuff!"

Troy took what cash Gregory had in his wallet, around three hundred dollars, and his credit cards. That would make it look like some prostitute had robbed him. He left the bag with the toys in the room, along with the mask. He donned a baseball cap and sunglasses and stuck his gloved hands into his pocket. He crept down the steps, glanced around and waited for the phone to ring at the front desk. When it did and the clerk turned his back, Troy hurried out the front door, quickly turning the corner and crossing the street.

A safe distance away, Troy spotted some garbage bins in an alley. He looked around then ditched the hat, the glasses, the gloves, and Gregory's credit cards into the garbage container. It wouldn't do to hold onto the cards. They could be traced. He didn't need them anyway.

A few hours later, he was on his way to Hawaii and feeling great. He had the money from the sale of the house in his bank book, the larger part of five-hundred-thousand dollars, and a message from his agent in LA saying she'd set him up with an agent in Hawaii. He had the world by the tail. And soon, very soon, he'd be living right down the beach from the man he loved more than anything in the world, the only man who'd ever given him exactly what he needed in bed and would be giving it to him again, every night . . . three and four times a night if he wanted it.

Nothing is more important to me than you, baby.

Four years ago, things had been very different. In trouble with the mob, suicidal, he needed to get rid of his life, so he handed it over to his twin brother. He never suspected the little twit would take to it like water and fall for his man. Troy had always intended to one day get back to Dave, get back to his life, then Aaron had stepped into it and wouldn't let go. Shit, things had not gone as planned. He'd hidden out, wanted by everyone . . . and not in a good way, and all the time he was running and hiding, that little slut brother of his was making love to his man, his lawful husband, lying in his bed, walking around in his shoes, his clothes.

So much for brotherly love!

One fateful night, Gregory Hill spotted Troy in a tavern in a rundown part of LA. At that time, Troy thought it was the end. The cop looked at him, recognition in his face, and Troy ran. He waited for Hill to catch up then jumped him in an alley. He took his gun and forced him to get behind the wheel of his police vehicle. He didn't know what to do with him, so he took him back to his run-down hotel room and tied him to the bed. He kept him there for days, considering his next plan of action and during that time, he began to discover a few things about the middle-aged detective he was sure no one else knew. It seemed the crueller he was to the man, the more abusive, the more the detective liked it. His cock hardened when Troy struck him and their relationship evolved into one where in exchange for some sexual domination, Gregory gradually became his willing slave in every way.

When Troy withheld his attentions, Gregory offered to do anything, to be anything, to receive them. It was perfect.

It had been easy for Troy to fake his own death, and when Gregory Hill's partner began asking too many questions, his body quickly substituted for Troy's. All it took was a few bribes to undertakers and coroners, and a shady character or two, all of which Gregory paid for out of his inheritance. And that was it. It was over. Even that crazy loan shark Aaron had been in debt to played along in exchange for a bundle of money.

Next, came months and months of plastic surgery. Sure, Troy had always been good looking, but with a few major changes . . . he no longer resembled his twin. He was more beautiful now, a tuck here, a nip there, and lots of time at the gym. All the pain had been worth it for freedom. Gregory helped secure him a new identity. There was nothing left of Troy Mayer now.

A few weeks after the healing, a Hollywood agent had walked right up to him on the street and asked to work for him. A year later, he was being offered jobs doing commercials. And as the plane flew over the Honolulu airport, he knew all had come together beautifully. Now it was time for the climax, and the happily ever after.

He had a career, he had money, and soon his husband would be back in his bed. He'd find a way to get rid of Aaron for good. Didn't mean he'd kill him. In fact, he might let him live, at least, so Troy could watch his dear twin suffer with a broken heart when he lost the man he loved. Maybe he'd let Dave fuck him while his brother Aaron watched. Now that was a satisfying fantasy.

Troy put himself up at the Halekulani Hotel for the night before moving on to Kauai. He'd contacted the realtor, sent her the payment online from his bank account, and was told he couldn't meet to sign the papers for his new house until the next day anyway. It was time for some rest and recreation. After he'd checked in to the hotel, he went looking for someone to share the room with. He was looking for something very specific. He had to be tall and well built, muscular and tanned, Latin descent . . . thick black hair and dark smouldering eyes.

He had to be David.

At the end, after talking up a few guys, he gave up. He didn't find him. Instead, he went back to the hotel alone, deciding that maybe it was time to start being faithful to his husband. He used his sex toys and imagined David beside him in the bed. He took the blown-up photograph out of his bag and pressed his lips to it. He fell asleep on it, jerking on his cock.

In the morning, he woke up with Dave's image beside him. He was ready to check out. He'd arranged to take a flight in. The realtor would meet him there with the keys. He kissed the paper face goodbye and began to tear it up into pieces. He no longer needed it. He was soon to have the real thing, flesh and blood, in his arms again.

"Don't worry, baby," he whispered, as he sprinkled the torn-up pieces into the garbage can. "I'm coming back to you. And this time, I'll be faithful. I promise."

He went down to the front desk and thanked the young woman for a wonderful night's stay. He paid his bill and left a generous tip for housekeeping.

"Please, come back again, Mr. Carlton." The young woman gave him a smile.

"Please call me Randy, pretty lady." He winked.

"Randy." She blushed a little.

"I'd love to come back but you see, I'm going to join my husband."

"He is a lucky man."

"I'm the lucky one," he said. "My husband is gorgeous. We've had a bit of a separation . . . some misunderstandings, but it's going to be all right now."

"I'm sure."

"I'd love to bring him here some time. Maybe we'll celebrate a second honeymoon. It should be soon. What do you think about renewing vows?"

"It's very romantic, and we do have a honeymoon suite." She giggled.

"I'll try to talk him into it. You know the other day he was just saying to me that we don't have enough time alone. He always wants to get me alone." He lowered his voice. "He can't get enough of me."

She smiled.

"Anyway, thanks again. Aloha!"

When Troy got outside, the sun was shining. *What a beautiful day,* he thought. He grabbed a taxi to the airport and took the twenty minute flight to Kauai. Kauai was the northernmost of the Hawaiian Islands, located about fifty miles off the coast of Oahu. They once had boat travel from the mainland but they'd stopped it, claiming it disturbed the wildlife and fish. Go figure!

An attractive young woman was there as he disembarked. She shook his hand. "Did you get the funds?" he asked anxiously. "I sent them last night by internet."

"Yes, and everything seems in order, Mr Carlton. I have the papers." She gave him an appreciative smile.

"Please, Randy."

"Randy. You can call me Alice."

They got into Alice's car. "I was a little surprised that you'd bought the place without visiting it first."

"I took the virtual tour. It seems wonderful. I really need a place where I can get some peace and quiet."

"You'll love it. You have made a good purchase. Wainiha, your section of Hanalei Bay, is quite remote. The nearest neighbours are a half mile away. A nice couple though."

"Really," Troy sat back in the seat as the car moved forward. *They aren't a couple. He's my husband, bitch!*

"The couple down the road," she lowered her voice and gave him a discreet look, "are two men . . . gorgeous. They have a bed and breakfast. David is a personal trainer. He's worked with celebrities. Sometimes he has to go off for a while, travels with them. Aaron, his partner, runs the place. They only get a few visitors. Aaron says it's nice having company when David is away. They have their separate quarters, of course, and they seem very much in love."

Fuck off! "Of course." Bed and breakfast? Um. How quaint!

"I don't blame Aaron for missing his husband. The man is . . . well . . . sorry to go on. My girlfriend saw him once and almost . . ." She chuckled. "I'm sure you're not interested. Anyway, they're quiet and cool . . . on the other side are your other neighbours, a mile down . . ."

He stopped listening at that point. Who cared about the other neighbors? Poor Aaron, all alone when David leaves on his trips with clients. His bed must seem so empty. Guess he can use a friend during those times, and he intended to be a good friend, to both of them, a shoulder and an ear.

They pulled up in front of Troy's new house, right on the beach front. "Here it is," the woman announced.

But he wasn't looking at his new property. His attention was completely captivated by something else—a tall, muscular man jogging in their direction, shirtless, with very short, blue nylon shorts and professional joggers.

"Mr. Carlton?" Alice said then followed his gaze. "Oh, well, there's Dave now." She waved. "Mr. Alvarez! Woo hoo! Come and meet your new neighbor." She looked at Troy.

Troy's heart was racing as he watched David walked over to them. His bronze skin gleamed with a delicious layer of sweat, his eyes . . . oh, those eyes . . . he was even more beautiful than Troy remembered.

Dave held out his hand and smiled. "Hello, I'm David Alvarez. I'm pleased to meet you."

Troy told himself to play it cool, but that smile, the touch of his hand, sent shock waves through him. "Randy Carlton. Nice to meet you, David."

"Randy just bought the old Fisher place here," Alice said, ogling David's chest.

Put your eyes back in your damn head, woman. He's gay and he's my husband!

"Great," David said. "It will be nice to have neighbors again. You on your own here, Randy?"

"Afraid so. I don't know anyone yet either."

"What do you do for a living, Randy?"

"I'm a model, an aspiring actor."

"Ah. Figures," he replied. Troy was pleased to see that Dave gave him a fast once-over. Oh, he was still very gay.

"You could be a model as well," Troy met his gaze and smiled. "You're gorgeous."

"Thanks." He gave him a brief smile. "I'm flattered but it's not for me, posing in front of cameras. I'm a personal trainer."

"So Alice told me. That's great. I could use a personal trainer. Are you for hire?"

David laughed.

It sounded like a sexual proposition but perfectly legit in context.

"Sure," Dave replied. "You can run with me sometimes. Aaron really doesn't like to run. He prefers to swim and surf."

"I'll do that," Randy said. "I'll run, for sure, but could I hire you for a personalised program. I have to keep in shape."

"Looks like you're doing a good job so far."

"Thanks for noticing." Troy met his gaze again.

"We'll work something out." David looked away.

"Perfect."

"First you'll have to come for a drink and meet Aaron."

"Love to. Just tell me when you want me." *Do you want me, David? Can't eat the same thing every night and not get a little itch once in a while, baby.*

"So, I'll let you get to it." David wiped his brow. "Welcome to the island." He glanced at Alice. "Nice to see you again, Alice." That thick, dark hair fell onto his forehead. It touched his shoulders, all that silky dark hair. He had let it grow longer. *Must be the island life bringing out the bohemian in him.* Troy liked it. He liked it a lot. He wanted to touch it, to kiss it.

Meanwhile, Alice was gushing all over herself as she said goodbye to Dave.

Troy kept his gaze on his delectable ass as Dave jogged off again. Alice was focused on his ass as well. *Could bounce pennies off of that ass and I could think of a lot more things I'd like to do with it.* Troy licked his lips thinking about it.

"My," Alice said, waving a hand in front of her face, "it got warm all of a sudden."

"I guess." Troy smirked.

"Let's go inside." She headed to the door. "He's such a nice guy."

"Yes, pity he's gay."

She glanced at Troy. "Oh, I didn't mean . . ."

Troy chuckled and followed her inside. *Didn't you, you bitch in heat?*

Alice showed him around, gave him his keys, and then, thank God, left him alone. Troy glanced around again. Bedroom, living room, kitchen, and bath. That's all he needed. It was fully furnished. He'd need a bigger bed. King sized. Dave liked big beds. He was tall, well over six foot, and he loved to stretch out. Yep. The bed had to go.

Troy took a chair and brought it outside. He sat down and waited. David had to jog back by here sometime. And sure enough, around twenty minutes later, his husband came running back up the beach. When he saw Troy outside, he lifted a hand but he kept on running. Troy waved back with a smile then looked up at the blue sky. He breathed in the fresh air. Yeah. All was as it should be. He was going to be just about the best neighbor these guys had ever had . . . best neighbor and best friend. He could bond. He closed his eyes and sighed with utter contentment.

CHAPTER TWO

Aaron often had bad dreams. They'd been getting worse lately. He dreamed that his evil twin, Troy, was still alive, and was coming to get him. The dreams were vivid and terrifying.

"I'm coming, Troy. Coming to get you. You whore!"

No, these weren't dreams. They were ugly, violent nightmares. He began to feel they were real. That Troy had somehow escaped death. But how?

He'd stopped telling Dave when he had the dreams because Dave became upset. He knew his husband hated seeing him in distress. It was much easier to pretend he wasn't having the horrific nightmares anymore. Aaron felt almost as if Troy wanted him to see him destroy people . . . things, such gruesome images he'd never experienced in life or sleep before he began to panic that Troy was alive and had just killed a man.

That's what Troy did. He destroyed.

Lives.

Aaron turned over in bed. He had forced himself to tell Dave he was too sleepy to swim. The truth had been worse. He'd been paralyzed from the terrible dream he'd had for the second night in a row. Of some guy trussed up in leather, Troy laughing as he slowly strangled the man.

The eyes. Oh, the pain, disbelief, the dreadful fear, and finally, hopeless acceptance as the poor man finally died.

He would never, ever forget the look in that man's eyes. It was too real to be a dream, but all the same, whatever it was, vision . . . hallucination, he wished it would stop. The dreams were so frequent and so disturbing he'd finally shared his secret with his chef and best friend, Genesis. She'd changed his diet completely and made sure he touched no alcohol.

But the dreams came anyway.

He thought back to the treacherous way his twin reached out to him after a long separation, offering him a new life. All the things he'd missed out on could now be his.

Yes, Troy had given him money and a means to change everything. He'd even given him a house and a car. And . . . Dave.

The dreams had started a few months ago. Up until then, everything had been perfect here in their little pocket of paradise. He and Dave were so happy, so compatible. Aaron knew it was crazy, but he felt that Troy resented losing Dave, the man he'd married and allegedly loved, but cheated on relentlessly. He'd also manipulated him, lied to him. He had hurt so many people.

That was the other thing Troy gave Aaron. Absolute hatred. Yes, he'd landed a big, beautiful house in the gated community of Bel Air, but all the neighbors hated Troy. Many of them, including his own household staff, were left shattered by his machinations. He'd tried to destroy Aaron's best friend Matt's life. When Aaron averted the plot and told Matt everything, Matt had beaten him severely.

The list went on.

There wasn't a single person Troy came near who came away unscathed. He was like a deadly Astrid in the garden. He wanted to take over. Control. And destroy. He poisoned people. Heck, he'd even poisoned one of his neighbor's trees back on St Cloud Road.

He shivered. He knew he should get up and start working. They had a house full of guests. He'd slept past his usual swim time. He knew Genesis would have breakfast on the table by now. He burrowed under the duvet, smelling his husband's scent.

Troy is dead. Dead, dead, dead.

He sighed and rose from the bed. He'd enjoyed the extra sleep time but knew by the end of the day his body would suffer for it. He needed to swim and surf the way Dave needed to run. He showered quickly and changed into a T-shirt and board shorts. Outside the house, he stuffed his feet into a pair of *zoris* kept near the front door and walked over to the bed and breakfast they'd created in the adjoining house.

Aaron paused to admire the rainbow in the sky, a hangover from the torrential rain overnight. He loved the rain. It was the reason the island was so verdant and lush. Kauai also had something the other islands didn't have.

Red dirt and dust. The red dirt permeated everything and stained the skin. He and Genesis cleaned the floors of the B and B constantly.

He smiled as he reached the stone stairs of the former *luna* cottage. Their houses had once ringed a pineapple field. The main house had belonged to the landowner, and the *luna*, or overseer, had lived in the second house. Both were huge, but people got a kick out of staying in the house that had once been a thriving part of island history. They had six guest rooms and two private bungalows farther down the slope of their property. Those were generally rented by honeymooners, or the occasional author who could spring for a private getaway to write.

Aaron kicked off his *zoris* and saw there were only a few pair beside his. That meant some of the guests had violated the house rules of no shoes in the house. It also meant red footprints everywhere.

He opened the door, stepped inside. *Yep. Red prints.*

Aaron heaved another sigh. Most of their guests were leaving today and a bunch of new arrivals were due. He and Dave would have two hours in which to clean and redress each room in time for their next batch of guests.

He could smell the heavenly scent of pancakes on the air and walked into the dining room, a smile across his face.

His guests lit up. Genesis was a whiz in the kitchen, but she didn't come and chat with their visitors. She left it to him and Dave to answer the same stupid questions about unprovoked shark attacks or where they could find jewelry to buy on the island of Kauai.

Aaron locked gazes with Rod, the young groom who'd booked and canceled the honeymoon cottage four times before Aaron gave it to him at a discounted price. It was clear Rod's wife, Wendy, wanted desperately to stay at Pineapple Hill, but they really couldn't afford it. Aaron believed in love and wanted to do something nice for the couple. What he hadn't known was that Rod was a dreadful Bible-basher who quoted Jesus way too often and pressed unwanted gifts of the Bible on everyone he came across. He'd also recorded a CD of his music.

It had been difficult to explain to Rod that people came to Kauai to relax and get away from stress. He and Dave had taken pains to explain it so that Rod understood that back on the mainland, people were punished with advertising. Punished each time they went to the grocery store by people wanting their money for charities, real and imagined.

At Pineapple Hill, they wanted people to rest and recuperate. Their rooms were their private sanctuary and leaving Bibles and cards with dire warnings on the edge of their beds was unacceptable.

"Aloha nui!" Wendy trilled. She was lovely. How she put up with mouthy Rod was anybody's guess.

"Wow, your Hawaiian is really good. A big aloha to you, too," Aaron said. He took a quick look around the table.

Genesis had done a wonderful job, as usual, with their breakfasts. It came as part of the room package, but Aaron knew she'd been a wonderful find. When he and Dave first started renovating the house to make a bed and breakfast hotel, she'd walked up to him on the beach. He'd seen her sleeping on it some nights and thought she might be homeless. Turned out she was just eccentric.

She loved to cook but hated constraint. She earned enough working for Aaron and Dave that she could survive, then played guitar on the weekends at a local bar. He and Dave couldn't believe the incredible sample breakfast she made for them. They hired her on the spot. Each morning she effortlessly turned out gourmet meals for their guests. Judging by the glowing reviews they got on Yelp and TripAdvisor, she'd become more than an asset. She was a necessity.

"You haven't played my CD yet and everybody wants to hear it," Rod whined. A few of the guests looked mortified. Nobody wanted to hear him recite the psalms on CD and hell-to-the-no listening to it over breakfast.

He caught a couple of pleading glances as he took a seat at the table. He cast an appreciative eye over the dazzling array of dishes Genesis had prepared. A cheese and asparagus strata, French toast made with fresh Portuguese bread, pancakes, and a platter off fresh island fruit.

"As soon as I've had a cup of coffee and a pancake, I'll play your CD," Aaron promised.

"Oh, no you don't," Genesis said, storming to the table. She placed a cup of tea and a bowl of the horrible organic grains she'd been making him eat ever since he'd told her about the dreams.

Who does she think she is? The food police?

"Yerba Mate. Nectar of the gods." She pointed to his green tea. When she'd first introduced herself to him that day on the beach, he'd thought she was a little bizarre with a name like Genesis, her bohemian clothing, and dreadlocked lilac-colored hair. He soon learned she was the warmest, most loving woman. At the age of thirty, she had boundless wisdom and an innate spirituality.

Still doesn't mean she's not as annoying as hell sometimes.

"Genesis, can you put my CD on?" Rod whined. Ever since he'd met her, the Jesus freak assumed she was one, too, because of her name. She'd made it clear the second they met that her parents named her after the band, not the first book in the Bible.

"My mother is a Phil Collins fan," she'd said.

A few people stopped eating, glancing up at her.

Aaron wished she'd go back to the kitchen. He was dying for a pancake. The guava and passion fruit sauce that came with it smelled so good.

"No," she said. "I let the guys handle the DJ chores." And with that she swished away, leaving a faint trail of *pikake* perfume in her wake.

Rod opened his mouth to protest. Albert, one half of a gay couple across the table, filled the small moment of silence with a question.

"We're heading to Maui today and since we have most of the day to fill until my parents arrive, I was wondering, should we go to Makawao?"

Aaron had more important things to ponder, such as how to get a cup of coffee into him. Fast. He'd have to get through the tea, he supposed, in order to replace it with coffee. He picked up his cup. The tea wasn't too hot, thank God.

Albert had mispronounced the name of the upcountry cowboy town. It wasn't Mack-cow-wow. It was Mack-a-wow.

"I think Makawao is gorgeous," Aaron said. "One of my favorite places in the islands. I know you and John love herbs and crystals. Unusual tinctures. The best place for that in all of Hawaii is the Dragon's Den."

Albert's face lit up. "You're the second person who's recommended that store. So we should really go there, I guess." He flicked a gaze at his husband's face. John was a lovely man. Even Rod, who'd at first balked at the idea of so many gay men on the property, acknowledged it was difficult to dislike a gay British pastor who had lost a leg protecting a little girl from an IRA bomb blast on the streets of London.

"I wish we could stay longer," John whispered. He had his good days and bad, but since he'd come to Pineapple Hill, he'd become so much stronger. He had color in his cheeks and his eyes shone. Genesis, Dave, and Aaron had come to treasure the man and doted on him. They didn't want the couple to leave either. They'd stayed for two weeks at a specially reduced rate, their first vacation since John had completed rehab. He was the only man among the group who truly had the Christian spirit. He not only tolerated but liked Rod, for one thing.

"Rod," he suddenly said, "could you please autograph your CD for me? I enjoy listening to it so much."

Aaron watched the way Rod's face transformed. He was so desperate for acceptance, poor man.

"Why, yes, of course!" He rushed off to his room.

"Quick!" said Steve, the mad surfer perched on the other end of the table. He'd come with his wife, Eileen, who hardly saw him. When he wasn't surfing, he was at one of the bars along the coast, avoiding her. Aaron and David wondered why they'd come here at all, since she wound up lying in their hammocks reading books most of the day.

"Let's go before he comes back and makes us all hold hands and pray," Steve said, scarfing down his last slice of toast. Aaron had to bite his tongue to stop himself from laughing. Steve and Eileen, who were also leaving that day, leapt from the table. When Rod returned with a batch of CDs, most of the guests, except for Albert and John, stood en-masse and left the table.

"More pancakes for me," Aaron said, forking one, then demolishing it quickly as the others talked. He had so much to do but first he had to eat a little of the icky gruel to keep Mama

Genesis off his back.

"Is it that bad?" John gazed at him kindly as he chewed.

Aaron nodded. "Don't tell her I said that."

He smiled. "Why does she have you on this regime. I'd kill for your figure."

"Aw, thanks," Aaron said. As Rod rushed off somewhere, John said, "I really wish we weren't leaving today."

"The feeling is mutual." Aaron sipped the last of the tea. "You do know you can always come back." Aaron glanced from him to Albert. "We've loved having you here. If you change your minds about Maui, we'll fit you in." He lowered his voice. "At the same rate."

"Thank you, Aaron." John looked emotional. He had a state-of-the-art prosthetic leg and walked with a cane. It had taken a lot of getting used to for the former triathlete. Dave and Aaron had loved being part of his recovery.

"We might take you up on it," Albert warned.

"I hope you do." Aaron drained his tea and stood, still desperate for a cup of coffee, but there was work to do. "Is there anything you need?" he asked them.

John shook his head. "Another week here would be bliss, but I have that wedding to officiate in Maui." He pulled a face. "A wedding here would be so lovely."

Aaron grinned. "Yes, it would."

Dave and Aaron had already met with a wedding planner who assured them that their establishment with both its rural aspect and ocean view would be perfect. Putting Pineapple Hill on the official register of places to get married in Hawaii had turned out to be expensive. So far, they'd held off forking out the small fortune. They had high hopes of spreading the word through satisfied customers.

"Do you mind if I relax on the sofa until we have to leave?" John asked.

"Of course not. Do you need help?" Aaron constantly

found himself asking John this question, but the man never complained. He was very self-sufficient and stood, making his way to the comfy lounge area.

"I'll go finish packing," Albert said.

"I'm so glad Rod and I have two more days here. I wish we could stay longer, too," Rod's wife said.

Aaron glanced at her. "So do I," he said. The truth was, he was counting the minutes until Rod left. He wondered why Wendy hated herself so much that she'd committed herself to a life of purgatory with him.

She smiled and left the room. Aaron began cleaning up the dishes. In the kitchen, he was shocked to find Genesis talking to a handsome man leaning against the sink as she loaded the dishwasher.

"Say, Aaron, have you met our new neighbor?" She straightened, pushing a curl of hair over her ear.

Aaron smiled and held out his hand. "Hi, I'm Aaron Alvarez." He noticed the small flicker of surprise crossing the other man's face as they clasped one another's hands.

"Randy Carlton. Pleased to meet you."

"Likewise." Aaron had the strangest, chilly sensation, like a weird electric shock the moment his fingers connected with Randy's. He pulled his hand back and found himself retreating. "You . . . um bought the old Fisher place?"

"Good guess." Randy smiled.

"Well, that's the only other place around here." Aaron heard the toot of a car horn. "Sorry to run but we have guests leaving. Nice to have met you."

"You, too, Aaron."

As he left the kitchen, Aaron felt completely off-kilter. He couldn't understand it. He shook it off. He had no time for drama. The first of the guests was leaving. Steve and Eileen were heading back home. Dave, who drove guests in the retired limo they'd bought as part of the package for their deluxe vacation deal, came up the stairs as Aaron was coming outside.

"There's a sight for sore eyes," Dave said, wrapping Aaron in a mighty hug and kissing him.

Aaron melted. Damn, he loved his husband. "I don't think I should be hob-nobbing with the likes of you, Sir," he teased, his smile a mile wide.

"I'll hob your knob the second I get home," Dave retorted. He turned at the sound of footsteps at the side of the house. It was their new neighbor.

"Hey," Dave said. "We meet again."

Randy nodded. "Just came to say hi. I see you're busy."

And they were.

"We're having a small drinks party here at six," Dave said. "Why don't you drop by? Nothing formal, just welcoming the new arrivals."

"I look forward to it," Randy said. He walked off.

Something about him really bothered Aaron but before he could say anything, Dave said, "I'll be back in an hour and fifteen minutes. Can you and Genesis have the cottage ready and the Hibiscus Room?"

"Of course." Aaron knew Dave liked it when Aaron was confident.

"Good. Then I'll expect your ass in our house for a quickie the moment I return."

Aaron blew him a kiss as Dave turned to help Steve and Eileen, who were lugging their possessions along the driveway. Like everyone else who came to paradise, they were leaving with far more than they'd arrived with.

He went inside, opened the utility closet hidden in the hallway, and picked up his cleaning kit. He left the house and walked along the path laden with tropical flowers to the cottage vacated by Steve and Eileen. He almost fell over. He dropped his bucket to the floor with a crash. What a mess.

They had virtually trashed the place.

"Holy shit," Genesis said, materializing by his side.

"I . . ." Aaron couldn't breathe. Nobody had treated their precious rooms this way. He thought of all the hours he and Dave had put into creating this romantic space. His cell phone rang. For a moment, he forgot he even had it on him. He checked the readout. Dave.

"Did they leave anything?" his husband asked. It was customary for Aaron to check wall plugs for cell phone and iPad adapters, the bathroom for forgotten toiletries, and even under the beds.

"They trashed our cottage," Aaron said. He wanted to call the police.

A pause. "Babe. I'm on my way."

He heard Dave running. Genesis, who was usually the one to jolly them out of any crisis point, clung to Aaron. She kept blinking.

"Holy shit." Dave walked in. He walked around, his mouth open in disbelief. He went into the bathroom, the bedroom, and came back out to the living room. "Okay, I'm going to tell them they've left this cottage in an unacceptable condition. We'll fix it as best we can, but we'll tell them we will get an estimate for the damage and charge their card."

"Okay." Aaron was conscious of breathing again.

Dave scratched his chin. "How in the world do you suppose they made all those scratches in the floor?"

Aaron shook his head. Their antique, original *koa* floors were rubbed by hand weekly. The vintage and also original bamboo blinds were broken.

The sofa cushions were torn and there were beer bottles everywhere. The sofa was stained.

"I'll go talk to them and make them sign a consent form," Dave said. He came over and hugged them both. "Make sure you take photos of everything first. I'll make them come in and look if they argue."

"Okay." Aaron followed Dave, still trying to absorb his shock. He retrieved the camera from the hall closet and returned to the cottage where Genesis still stood where he'd left her.

"You think we can make it habitable for that author who's coming to stay?"

"Yes," Aaron said, laying his cell phone on the entry table. He began taking photos. Romance author Jerry Race had booked the cottage for a week. He was using Kauai as the location in his latest book and wanted to soak up the atmosphere.

Aaron felt wretched. Mr. Race seemed like such a nice man and had been so excited to stay here. Aaron's cell phone rang.

"I'll get it." Genesis reached for it. "Dave," she announced, taking the call. Aaron processed the rooms, aware that he'd known this day would come but had always hoped it wouldn't.

"You're kidding," he could hear Genesis saying. She came to the bathroom, which was the only room not left in tatters. "Dave says they don't recall ripping the blinds or the sofa. They say they did drink quite a bit but have no idea how these things happened. They also say they don't know where the scratches came from. They said the scratches weren't there when they checked out of the cottage. They won't pay any fees for damages."

"Then I guess we'll be black-listing them," Aaron said.

"You betcha bippy," she said. She talked into the phone and Aaron finished taking photos. He had no hesitation in contacting the tightly connected group of Bed and Breakfast owners in the islands. Their network was competitive but supportive and frequently shared tips about bad visitors or equally, referred business to one another.

Genesis came back to him. "I'll start on the Hibiscus

Room," she said. "Can you handle this?"

"Yes," he said, determined to make this visit the one of Mr. Race's dreams. He cleaned frantically, throwing bottle after bottle into the empty trash bag he'd brought in his kit. He emptied and re-lined the waste baskets in the room, stripped the bed, and removed the towels, stowing them in his laundry bag.

He had a system and it worked. He restocked the cottage's linen closet with all the things he and Dave provided for their guests. Steve and Eileen had souvenired all the island ginger hand soaps, as well as the skin and hair care products. He counted the linens. They'd also swiped a few towels.

Aaron ran back and forth to the washing machine and the storage rooms where he kept extra supplies. After scrubbing the tub and bathroom sink, he replaced all the soaps and toiletries in the bathroom then started work on the *koa* floor. He slathered a thick layer of the special wood paste Genesis had created for him into the worst areas and let it set. He then began to focus on the areas that just required a light cleaning and sprucing. He could tell the deep scratches that almost looked like claw marks weren't improving and tried not to panic.

He stared at the pattern for a moment. It was as though some wild animal had broken in here and run amok, but he knew they hadn't. There weren't any wild animals out here. Only their paying guests.

After finishing all the cleaning except for the worst of the floor areas, he finally made the bed and made sure it was exactly as he liked it. He placed a batch of the chocolate and island coconut candies he and Genesis made each week into the empty candy dish on one side of the bed and, on the other, a pair of the flip flops he and Dave gave each visitor as a welcome gift. Aaron handmade each pair, thanks to a local store, where customers could choose their own adornments.

For Mr. Race, Aaron had selected a metallic typewriter that the writer could also use as a magnet if he so chose. The final touch was a vase full of orchids that matched the ones he left on each pillow. He checked his cell phone. Thirteen minutes until Dave came home with Mr. Race.

And his demands for a quickie.

Aaron got to his knees and rubbed the scratches. Miracle of miracles, the paste had worked after all. He buffed furiously until the floor shone. Only one thing left to do—repair the torn blind and replace the sofa cushions.

He hated throwing out the cushions he and Dave had found at arts and crafts fairs, but he had a few duplicates in storage. The blind would need to be repaired but in the meantime he removed it and improvised a curtain with a piece of vintage Duke Kahanamoku silk he tied off with a sage green ribbon. Actually, it worked, and Aaron took one more critical walk around the cottage, before closing the door.

Inside the house, Genesis had finished one room and started on another. He really wanted to make the beds and tidy the house, but Dave came first.

"I'll be back," he called out to her and ran next door. He'd barely made it inside when he heard the car pull up front. He heard voices. Genesis took custody of their visiting writer as Aaron kicked off his shorts. He was so excited about a quickie with Dave his cock sprang to attention as Dave ran through the door.

"You're not ready," Dave growled, tackling Aaron to the floor. "Mmmm . . . you smell of guava and jasmine, baby."

Aaron gasped as Dave began kissing and licking his face and throat. "Yeah. The floor paste. It's good stuff. It . . . works." His cock began leaking in Dave's hand as his husband got between Aaron's legs. Aaron wanted his man so badly he couldn't see straight.

"Fuck me," he said. "Make it snappy."

Dave grinned down at him. "My bossy husband." He lifted Aaron's legs, licked at his ass cheeks and then began sucking his hole. Aaron's whole body trembled. He loved their long, luxurious lovemaking sessions, but thank God, he'd married a man who knew how to fuck good and hard when the occasion arose.

And in their relationship, it arose a lot.

Dave lowered Aaron's body, undid his fly, and his cock sprang out. Aaron lifted his hips to meet the luscious shaft straining for him and reached down to push Dave's running pants below his knees. Dave entered him, pressing his cock with measured strokes. Aaron moved with him, rolling his hips, a silent 'please,' on his lips. Dave pumped harder and faster, Aaron's cock in his strong grip.

"Yeah. That's it. God you feel so good." Dave's entire length sank into him and Aaron thought he might break in half, but heck, what a way to go. Without much preparation, Dave's cock was almost too huge, but Aaron, as usual, quickly adapted. They fucked each other with complete abandon, Dave stroking Aaron to a strong orgasm. He shot deep inside Aaron, a look of total surrender on his face.

Aaron loved that look on his man.

Too soon, they got up from the floor and cleaned up, racing back to the house. Dave had to grab the shopping list from Genesis, who had the rest of the day off. She always finished work after the morning rush.

He would drop off the last guests leaving that morning, and Aaron would work on cleaning the common areas and the last guest room, Plumeria, which mercifully required just cleaning and fresh sheets. Once again, he ran through his checklist of all the extras they provided for their clientele. The mystery man who'd booked this room wouldn't give them his name. He'd booked through Pleasant Holidays and his package included a rental car.

I wonder who the hell he is and what the big mystery is. He can't be some big movie star. He would have booked a cottage.

Aaron heard the car drive up as he gave the room one final critical once-over and grabbed a fresh *plumeria lei* from the fridge, then walked outside to greet their guest.

"My God! Nikko!" Aaron shouted with joy at the welcome sight of their former neighbor from Bel Air. Nikko Watanabe, a TV actor, had stayed in touch with Aaron and Dave who had rented out their house back in LA. He hugged Aaron hard. When Dave came around the corner with John and Albert's luggage, he dropped the bags and hurried to their friend, who gave him a hug too.

Nikko stared at them. "Married life in paradise suits you," he said. "Man, it's good to see you!"

Aaron bid him an *Aloha* and gave him his *lei* greeting, slipping the fragrant flowers over Nikko's head and around his neck. Quickly hugging John and Albert goodbye, a strange feeling of panic enveloped him as he took Nikko to his room. The actor raved over the sumptuous island furniture, the vintage bric-a-brac, and the flip flops with a samurai sword embellishment.

"The agent at Pleasant Holidays said you love samurai stuff. I never guessed it was you!" Aaron said.

Nikko laughed. "I swore her to secrecy. I love this attention to detail. It's so you!"

It *was* him. Aaron loved taking care of their guests.

"I want to try new things this trip." Nikko leaned back, relaxing in the big wing chair by the windows. "I've been reading about Kipu Falls. Do you recommend them?"

Aaron stifled a groan. He loved people exploring his precious island, but he hated that visitors had begun finding out about secret places in the islands thanks to an irresponsible collection of books the locals disparagingly called The Blue Book. The authors not only gave detailed directions to hidden gems that only locals had been privy to, but apparently didn't care that many required trespassing on private property.

The outer islands were filled with people who were a bit, well, quirky, who prized their solitude and the untouched splendor of Kauai above all else. Suddenly they were being subjected to hundreds of people each and every week parading through their properties to get to 'hidden Kaui.'

Aaron and Dave had heard all the stories and tried to discourage their guests from partaking of illegal activities. Kipu Falls in particular was a raw wound. Two young women had read The Blue Book and had come to the garden island and followed the directions to it. They saw a trespassing sign at the main dirt road and chose an unmarked path instead. Within seconds, they had no idea they were on the edge of an obscured cliff and fell to their deaths.

Their parents had come to Kauai, grief stricken. Aaron would never forget the pain and suffering he saw in their faces.

"It's dangerous," he told Nikko. "Ten people have died there."

"So I've heard." Nikko's gaze held a defiant gleam. *Oh, boy.*

"And Queen's Bath. What do you know of it?"

"You have to be a strong swimmer. The tides are rough. We've had a few tragedies there, too."

"I love a challenge." Nikko grinned at him. Aaron returned his smile, left Nikko to his own devices, and went to the living room, straightening it one more time. In the kitchen, he sat at the table making a list of the canapés he would serve with drinks. Since Dave was picking up a lot of stuff they needed, he would wait before preparing anything.

In the meantime, he checked emails, made notes of their new reservations. They had bookings through the New Year. He checked Yelp and TripAdvisor for their customer reviews. Nothing he needed to respond to. Yet. He wondered what the heck Steve and Eileen would say.

That reminded him. He signed onto the Yahoo group he

and the other B and B owners had formed and warned them about the couple. *I have photos,* he posted. *I'll put them in the database later.*

He shut down the computer and walked along the path outside to Mr. Race's room. He knocked on the door, introduced himself, and prepared to apologize if the man had noticed any discrepancies with what he'd seen online versus the actual appearance of his accommodations.

The author was effusive in his praise and said, "I never, ever want to go home."

They all said that, and it was balm to Aaron's anxious state. After Mr. Race assured him he had everything he needed, Aaron continued on his way and walked past Rod and Wendy's cottage where he could hear the religious CD playing. Rod played it all day long.

Aaron crossed over to his herb and salad garden, cutting and pulling what he needed for their little drinks party that night. He and Dave only provided breakfast but as a personal gesture of hospitality, kept chilled, homemade coconut water and chilled cucumber water available for their guests in the dining room. It was another one of their little touches their visitors raved about.

He was in the kitchen a couple of hours later, cleaning and organizing food, when Dave arrived, saying, "Can I kidnap my husband for a quick lunch?"

Aaron laughed. "Of course you can." He helped Dave stow the food in the fridge and pantry and walked outside, slid his *zoris* onto his feet, and got into the car.

They held hands the whole way to the Ching Young Village. They loved the sushi bar there, but as they entered the sweeping shopping center with its vintage-looking red roofs, he thought about how they used to tear around the island to get their tasks accomplished. They'd learned the art of slow shopping here. It was a way of life.

"Mind if we take a quick look inside the Flop Shop?" he

asked.

"Nope. I never mind," Dave said, as they went inside. Aaron checked their new arrivals and picked up the few sizes of flip flops missing from his stash, plus a few new embellishments. He was astonished when he approached the service desk to see the new neighbor—what was his name . . . Randy—talking to Dave.

"Hello again," Aaron said.

Randy smiled. "I have almost no food and thought I'd come and check this place out. Your chef told me this is the place to go—that I'd find anything I wanted here."

Aaron felt a chill go through him. Why was Randy looking at Dave when he said that? Aaron saw the crimson flush on his husband's face. *It's not my imagination. He's making a pass at my husband!*

Dave insisted on using his credit card for Aaron's purchases and after an awkward silence, the two men left the store.

"See you this evening!" Randy trilled.

I do not like that man," Aaron said when they were out of hearing.

"Randy? Oh, he's harmless."

Aaron didn't say anything. There was something about Randy Carlton that just really set him on edge.

"Sweetie, are you jealous?" Dave pulled him to him and gave him a quick kiss. "Don't be. I love you to bits. And besides, he seems really rather sweet. I guess he'll keep you on your toes."

Aaron turned and found the man not far behind them. Is he following us? When he saw Randy walk into a coffee shop, he let out a breath.

I'm too suspicious. I gotta calm down. Dave's right. He's just lonely and needs friends. He hugged Dave back and tried not to worry, tried not to stress. He looked back over his shoulder, relieved to find that his creepy new neighbor was nowhere in sight.

CHAPTER THREE

It was difficult to describe what a sublime pleasure it was for Troy to look into his husband's eyes and hear his deep, smooth voice responding to him as they spoke. His slut brother was entertaining the author and that annoying ex-next door neighbour of his. Yes, *his* neighbour. Him. Oh, and the old fart that had lived on the other side. Him and his fucking tree. Troy had poisoned the damn thing once, should have taken an axe and chopped the damn thing in half while he was at it. What in hell was Nikko doing here anyway?

"So . . ." Dave's attention left Troy and focused on the author all of a sudden." What do you write, Jerry? I'm sorry I don't have a lot of time for reading."

Only because my twin is like a bitch in heat. Troy noticed Jerry checking Dave out. Hell, it seemed everyone in the room wanted to fuck his husband. And how dare Aaron take Dave's last name! *What a pussy.*

"Ah, gay erotic fiction actually. You'd make a great character in my next book," Jerry said to David. "Would you consider posing for the cover?"

Dave laughed. "I don't think . . . I . . ."

"Do it," Aaron urged, coming over and sitting on Dave's knee. He kissed his mouth quickly then snuggled down beside him. "You're so good-looking."

Troy held back the urge to gag. *Fucking whore, slut to the ninth degree. Leave him alone five minutes, Aaron. Let the guy breathe.* He'd never let Dave pose for anyone except himself. What was that twin of his thinking, giving David permission to do shit like that? Did he want to encourage stalkers?

"Flattering." David laughed. "But I don't think so."

"Dave, you're gorgeous," Nikko said. "I'd be flattered as hell."

Then you do it, jack off!

"I'm flattered but . . ." David trailed off.

"He doesn't have to pose naked, does he? That I wouldn't much care for." Aaron looked anxious.

Moron. You started this. Get a brain. How could this twit be my twin? The liberties he's taking with my husband who is only on loan . . .

Jerry shook his head and chuckled. "Don't worry . . . only shirtless on the beach maybe? I want to write a story set here. It's so beautiful."

"I could take the pictures," Troy volunteered, as Nikko agreed with Jerry's hype about the beauty of the island.

"I'm a bit of a photo buff," he added.

David turned to look at him. "Oh yes?"

Aaron gave Troy the dirtiest look. "We'll have them done by a professional."

"I was just trying to be nice," Troy murmured, looking wounded. It had the right effect. David frowned at Aaron.

Aaron shrugged but he looked hurt. He abruptly turned his attention to Troy's ex-neighbour.

David was brought up to be polite, and he was well mannered. Troy knew he didn't like rudeness. He was always on Troy's case in the past whenever he thought he'd forgotten his manners in public. Poor, poor Aaron. Troy might as well get some more mileage out of this one.

"I need some air," he told Dave and got up to walk outside.

David followed. Troy smiled. He knew his man so well. Dave had a big heart, didn't like seeing people sad or upset. He was about to apologise for his slut of a partner.

"I'm sorry," Dave said. "Aaron had a shitty day. We both did."

41

"Oh no," Troy said touching Dave's well-muscled forearm. "What happened?"

"Someone trashed one of the rooms. And the guests who were in it refused to pay. They said they didn't do it."

"Some people." Troy shook his head. It had taken minutes to trash that room. So easy to upset his poor brother. "They don't want to take responsibility for their actions. Anything I can do to help?" *Can I suck your cock for you, baby? How about you fuck me until I scream?*

"No, thanks. It's under control."

"I found Aaron overreacted a little to my suggestion. He seems really . . . I don't know . . . clingy sometimes. Is he always that insecure? You didn't cheat on him in the past or anything, did you? Oh shit, David, I spoke out of turn."

"No, it's okay, and I didn't cheat on him. He's usually not like this."

My sweetie is frowning.

"I've taken some photography classes, thought I'd save you a few dollars and that nice author, too, but . . . I'll mind my business from now on."

"Randy, it was a nice gesture. Thanks. But I'm no cover model."

"David." Troy looked at him, meeting those beautiful eyes. God, David made him so hard just looking at him. "You've got the body of a god and the face of an angel."

Dave cleared his throat. "Yeah well . . . thanks," he said hastily. "We better get back in there."

Aaron came outside. "David? What's going on?"

Oh good, brother. Just perfect, act all suspicious and jealous. David hates that shit.

"Nothing," David replied. "Although I think you hurt Randy's feelings a little." David smiled indulgently at Aaron.

"No, it's okay," Troy shook his head. "Really. I was out of line."

Aaron reached out and pulled David closer. That was for

Troy's benefit. He wanted to show him just who David belonged to. "Well, didn't mean to . . ." Aaron began then stopped. "Sorry," he muttered, but he didn't mean it at all. He looked right at David. "Coming in?"

David nodded, pulled away from Aaron, and went back inside.

Troy smiled at Aaron. "I want to be your friend. I hope we're not starting off on the wrong foot. I was just trying to help. I realise a professional would be much better if David was going to do it."

"Well, he's not." Aaron shook his head. "No worries. I overreacted, I guess. Just one thing, Randy, David is mine." He met Troy's gaze. "I want to be clear about that."

"Aaron," Troy laughed. "I admit David is hot as hell but really . . . listen." He put up his hands. "I have a confession."

Aaron waited.

"I just came out of a pretty bad breakup."

"Oh." His expression softened. "Really?"

"Um." Troy nodded, forcing the tears to his eyes. "He was . . . abusive."

"Oh God, I'm sorry," Aaron said. "Did he hurt you?"

"He tried to kill me."

Aaron's eyes widened.

"I was the submissive in a . . . BDSM thing. It was his trip. I went along with it because I loved him. And he tried to strangle me in a hotel room." He sobbed into his hands. "I almost died. I can still feel the scarf tightening around . . ." Troy choked and looked as if he was pulling it together. He wiped at his eyes.

Aaron placed a hand on his shoulder. Troy moved away from him. "Don't tell David about this, okay?"

"I won't. I'm so sorry. Where is he now, this . . . boyfriend?"

"I don't know. I get scared sometimes at night, dream he's

looking through my window."

"I have bad dreams, too. Not . . . easy."

Troy sniffed. "No. Guess I'm a little jealous of you and David. You have what I've always wanted, and with a real man like David who's strong and good and kind. David loves you so much."

Aaron got misty eyes. "I'm sorry. I won't . . . I mean, I know you meant well in there. I'll . . . go in. When you're ready, come and join us, okay?"

Troy nodded, smiling. "Thank you. It's nice to have a friend."

Aaron nodded and disappeared inside. Troy looked up at the starry sky. A little while later, he joined the gang. He stayed for a bit then decided it was time to go. "I need to leave," Troy told Aaron. "Thanks so much for everything. I have to be up early tomorrow."

Aaron gave him a sympathetic look. "I'll walk you home if you like."

"You're just so nice, Aaron. No, really. I'll ah . . . go on my own. I'll be all right. Thanks," he said, squeezing his arm.

Troy left, walking leisurely down the beach, humming a little song. And in the distance, he saw Genesis. The beginning of Genesis came to his head — not the rock group, the Bible, and he found himself reciting it.

"In the beginning God created the Heavens and the Earth. Now the Earth was formless and empty, darkness was over the surface of the deep, and the Spirit of God was hovering over the waters. And God said, 'Let there be light,' and there was light. God saw that the light was good, and he separated the light from the darkness. God called the light 'day,' and the darkness he called 'night.'"

"Randy?" Genesis gasped, looking up from where she sat on the beach.

He'd startled her. "Hey there."

"Were you reciting the Bible?"

"Was I?" He laughed. "Didn't think I'd said all that aloud. Mind if I join you?"

"No, feel free," she invited, passing Troy the bottle of wine she had cradled between her knees.

Troy plunked down in the sand beside her, took the bottle and swigged some. *Cheap wine.* "Thanks." He passed it back. "Nice evening."

"Yes, sometimes I like to sleep out here."

"Aren't you afraid?" He looked at her.

"No. Of what? It's perfectly safe here."

"I would be nervous out here all alone. Never can tell who wanders this stretch of beach of night." Troy made a scary face.

She laughed.

"Look at those stars." He pointed.

"Um. The moon is beautiful."

"A lover's moon. Only my lover is with another tonight."

"Oh, I'm sorry." She looked at Troy.

"It's okay," he said. "No worries. It's soon to be remedied. One night I'll be out here looking at this sky with him."

"Really? Is he married and getting divorced or something?"

"Well, not really. It's complicated. You see, David is my husband."

She laughed. "Did you say David, not . . . Aaron's David?"

Anger rose in him. "Aaron's David?" His voice trembled. "He's not Aaron's David, you fool! He's mine."

Her eyes widened. She started to get up. "I have to go. I . . ."

Troy held her arm and kept her on the ground. "You know, it's unfortunate you being here. I need to get close to my lover. Aaron has had my life for long enough now. I can't stand him touching David. I'm going quite mad."

Genesis began to struggle then to scream but he covered her mouth and took her around the neck. Pressing her back in the sand, Troy squeezed her throat hard and looked down into her startled eyes as the wine poured into the sand.

"God saw that the light was good, and he separated the light from the darkness. God called the light 'day,' and the darkness he called 'night.' Poor, poor Genesis. She's had too much to drink. The tide coming in can be a bitch. Ashes to ashes . . . dust to dust."

Troy picked up her limp body and carried her up the beach, along with her empty bottle. He watched as Genesis and her bottle floated out on the waves. Very poetic. "You gotta to be careful about hanging out on beaches at all hours of night. Didn't your Momma teach you anything, girl-friend?"

Troy went back to his little house after that and took off all his clothes. He lay on the bed and stroked his cock a while, picturing Dave naked on a book cover. Yeah, he could take Dave's picture. In fact, he still had pictures. Troy got out of bed and pawed through his bag. He took out several naked pictures he'd taken of Dave on their honeymoon. God, the camera loved him. Troy focussed on Dave's chest, so muscular with those taut, dark nipples and his cock, much larger than most men could even pray for, and inside Troy's ass . . . that cock had been a pleasure unsurpassed.

He stroked himself as he examined the pictures. "Mine," he whispered. "Take me, David. Fuck me, baby. Fuck me . . . yeah . . ." Troy came in his hand, kissed each picture then turned over and went to sleep. He had to be up early if he was going to jog with David. Too bad Aaron wasn't a jogger. Too, too bad.

First thing in the morning, Troy had a message from his agent. She could wait. He took a shower and looked at his face in the mirror. He looked well rested . . . he looked fantastic. He'd slept like a baby. He put on short shorts, a muscle top, and some good running shoes. He tied his hair back and waited for David. "Feast your eyes on this, baby," Troy murmured, as he walked outside, stretching a bit, waiting for David to come running by.

When Troy saw him, he jogged up to meet him. The sky was blue, and the sun was shining. The faint breeze was Heaven. "Hey there!"

David smiled. "Hey."

Troy began running beside him. He slowed down some for him to catch up. What a sweetie. *When David comes back to my bed though, he won't be out jogging at his hour.* Troy would make sure he was busy with his cock so far up his ass David would never want to take it out again.

"So, you got to make me a personal program, remember?"

"Sure," he said. He sped up a bit. Troy knew he would. David was a fitness nut. When you saw him naked you appreciated it but still, if he had to tie David to the bed when Aaron was out of the way, he would just to keep from doing this shit every day.

"Man, you run fast." Troy was breathing hard.

"Sorry." He laughed, turning around and jogging on the spot.

He completed the run with David, barely, and finally, mercifully, David stopped. They sat on a bench and drank some water.

"How you doing?" David asked Troy, wiping his chest on a towel. He stood up and stretched a bit.

Yum. Troy was distracted for a minute then he remembered. "Oh, you heard?"

"Heard what?"

Troy couldn't help watch that towel moving over his chest. "I thought Aaron would have told you." He got to his feet, reached out, and took the towel from him. "Let me get your back." Troy didn't wait for his answer, just moved around and wiped the towel across his broad shoulders then down his back to that delicious ass. He had to step back not to reach out for those two hard, round globes. Troy came around front and handed David back the towel.

"What's going on?" David persisted.

"I was telling Aaron about my ex. He tried to kill me."

"Shit."

"Um." Troy nodded. "Want to get a drink?"

"I got to get back. Genesis never showed this morning, and we got guests to make breakfast for."

"Really? You need a hand? I'm a pretty good cook."

"Yeah?" Dave lifted an eyebrow. "Really?"

"I'm in between jobs. I'd be happy to help out. Just until Genesis returns, of course, and I'd work for free."

"No, we'd pay you." David grinned. "Let's get back. Aaron will be relieved."

When they got there, Aaron was in a titter. "It's not like Genesis," he was saying, not making too much of a fuss about Troy's offer to help out. "I really appreciate this, Randy. Can you cook?"

"Can I cook?" He grinned. "My father was a chef." *Dad was actually in import and export business, but what the hell. Close enough!*

"Perfect," Aaron said.

David gave Aaron a quick kiss. "See, told you all would work out. I'm going to rinse off then I'll be down to help."

"Look," Troy said to Aaron, his gaze following Dave as he disappeared. God, he could picture being in the shower with David, the water running over his body. Troy licked his lips and told himself to concentrate. "I don't want you to worry." He managed to focus again on Aaron. "Just let me take a quick shower here, and I'll get to work. The guests aren't up yet, right?"

"No, you got time," Aaron said. "Let me show you where the guest showers are."

"Just point the way. I'll find it," Troy told him.

"Up the stairs to your right," Aaron said.

"Right." He nodded. "The left is your quarters."

Aaron nodded. He chewed on his nail a minute, distracted. "I don't get it. She's never been late. She's not answering her phone."

"She was a bit of a ... hippie ... right? You know those types. Look, I'm going to do the shower fast, be right back." Troy smiled at him, touched his arm. "Don't worry. You'll get frown lines."

He raced up the stairs and glanced down the hallway. Troy could hear the water running. He leaned against the wall and rubbed his cock. *David. I will devote the rest of my life to us. I have been a fool. I'm back. Sweetheart. I'm yours. I'll never so much as look at another man again.*

Troy drew closer, opening the door that separated the B and B from the rest of the house. The bedroom door was open. He walked in. The first thing Troy saw was a king-sized bed, *their* bed. He wanted to vomit on it, shit on it. He took a breath. The bathroom door was open. The sound of running water stopped. Troy walked in. David stepped out of the shower and Troy stood there, frozen, savouring the sight of his naked husband. Troy had a right to see him naked, the right to touch him anywhere he wanted.

David looked disgruntled. He grabbed a towel and wrapped it around his waist. "Randy! What the fuck!"

"Oh my God." Troy put a hand to his mouth. "I'm so sorry. Aaron must have told me the wrong way, or I probably got it wrong. He said I could take a shower. This isn't the guest shower, is it?"

"No." David shook his head. "It isn't."

"I'll go and find it." The water gleamed on David's tan skin, drops shining like diamonds, perfect drops to catch on

49

the tip of his tongue. Troy wanted to touch his tongue to the tips of those nipples, make them harder, suck them . . . and then his cock . . . David's cock. He wanted to fuck David suddenly, tie him up, make him cry out his name.

"Randy?"

Troy blinked, turned to see Aaron standing there. "I took the wrong way." He shook his head. "Where is the shower?"

Aaron wasn't happy with Troy's little misdirected path. He could tell. There was silence. David was the one who finally gave Troy directions, and he quickly left the room. He waited outside to hear Aaron say exactly what he thought he'd say.

"What the fuck is going on here?"

"Nothing," David replied. "He got lost."

"Lost?"

"Yeah."

"And you naked in the shower."

"Aaron, do you expect me to shower with my clothes on?"

There was silence. *Come on,* Troy silently urged, *argue, fight. David never did like jealousy tantrums. It bores him because, stupid boy, David would never, ever cheat on you, even if you weren't giving him any. He's far too honourable for that.*

"You're so hot," Aaron groaned suddenly.

Fuck! Oh no, fight, damn it.

"Take off that towel," Aaron demanded. "I want to look at you, fondle you a minute."

"We don't have time," David replied.

It didn't convince Troy.

"Come on, David. Please. I just want to play with it."

Silence.

Come on, David, kick him out. Tell him off.

"Um, Dave, it's so big . . . shit . . . you're hard, baby. Wish you had time to fuck me. God, I want to be fucked by you."

"Um . . . Aaron . . . ah . . . stop, baby . . . stop. You gotta cook, and . . ."

"So hot . . . so hot . . . um . . . David, please."

"Suck it. Suck it . . . .um . . . gonna fuck your face . . ."

Troy swallowed hard. He hit the wall with his fist then re-treated to the guests' showers. Troy felt as if he could kill him. *I could kill Aaron now.* He told himself to calm down. "David will be mine." He showered quickly, pulled shorts on, and ran downstairs.

Troy got to the kitchen and began to think about what he would make for breakfast. He'd left the shirt off, rubbed his own nipples a little before he came down, making them hard. Troy's cock was hard, too, as he took out the eggs. He'd make omelettes. He was good at it. He broke the eggs, thinking about Aaron's head. Each minute that went by, he thought about his brother up there with his husband.

When Troy heard David come down, he turned and gave his nipples a quick pinch again. David had always liked his nipples, and he could suck and twist them like none other. Troy turned from the fridge. "Hey." He smiled.

David's eyes zeroed in on Troy's chest a minute then looked away. How could he not? "Hope you don't mind me without my shirt. I . . . I'm hot." Troy met David's eyes.

David just smiled. "It's warm today. What are you mak-ing?"

"Omelettes."

"Great," Dave replied.

Aaron came into the kitchen. Troy could have slapped that smug smile off his face. He grabbed David and hung all over him a minute. They kissed then separated. "You know," Aaron said, pouring himself coffee, "I tried Genesis again. No answer. I'm worried now."

"Maybe she hooked up," Troy offered.

Aaron shook his head. "Not like her."

"Try not to worry, baby," David said, taking a cup of coffee from Aaron. "The guests are up now. Think I'll bring them coffee and entertain."

"Good idea," Troy said. "Aaron can help me here."

Aaron glanced at him. "I'll make toast."

"Good. We'll keep them on the warmer. So," Troy said, preparing the omelette pan, "you and David seem so . . . happy. Where did you meet him?"

Aaron froze.

Troy smiled. He knew that question would throw him.

"I'm sorry, I didn't mean to pry." *Could it be you just moved in on my fucking life, bitch, and took over?*

"We ah . . . met in Los Angeles."

"He's a great find. So . . . masculine . . . strong . . . hot. Is he good in bed?" Troy looked at Aaron.

Aaron's mouth opened.

"Come on . . . you're no prude. Just between girlfriends . . . is he good with his cock? Fucks you nice and deep?"

"We're not . . . girlfriends," Aaron said, meeting Troy's gaze. "I thought I made it clear about David."

"I'm not after David," Troy shook his head, beating the eggs. "You know my sad history."

"What made you walk in on him in the shower then?"

"It was an accident, Aaron. I'm sorry. I . . . he's yours. He's in your bed every night fucking you, isn't he?"

Aaron didn't reply.

"Should we add mushrooms?"

"Just plain," Aaron replied.

"Listen, again, don't mind me. I'm lonely since my ex left. Even if he did try to kill me, I loved him."

"How could you love someone who tried to kill you?" Aaron asked.

"He was a great fuck. You'll do a lot for great sex, wouldn't you?"

Aaron nodded. "I guess."

"So," Troy heaved a sigh, flipping his masterpiece, "was it love at first sight with you two?"

"No . . . not exactly." He was buttering toast.

"Tell me your secret?"

"Secret?" Aaron raised his brows.

"How does a man like you keep someone like David satisfied in bed?"

"What do you mean by . . . a man like me?"

"Hey, Aaron, let's not kid ourselves, look at him." Troy motioned through the partition. David was sitting at the table talking with Jerry and Nikko. "That's a real man . . . and you . . . well . . . you're not that experienced in bed, are you? He could have any guy he wanted. David must find himself wanting more sometimes . . . thinking about fucking other guys. It's quite normal."

Aaron's jaw worked. "I don't think . . . David wants . . . needs any other guy."

"Good. Well," Troy smiled at him. "Breakfast is ready."

Aaron was quiet though breakfast, probably pondering what Troy had told him. *Insecure much?* Troy lavished some attention on the writer, asking him about his latest book. No writer in the world could ignore that kind of attention. "So, tell us, Jerry," he flirted some, giving him a winning smile as Troy stirred his coffee, "what's the sexiest scene you've ever written or wanted to?"

"Breakfast table may not be the best place for that," Jerry replied. He looked like he was blushing. Troy nudged him. "Come on, I'm curious. You guys don't mind, right?" He looked around. "Come on, Jerry, how often do we get a real writer who writes hot man on man action? And I'm sure you write from real experience?"

"Well," Jerry shrugged. "I find light bondage sexy."

"Light?" Troy wrinkled his nose. "Come on. Give Aaron and David some ideas. They don't want their sex life to get boring." He laughed.

Aaron didn't laugh.

David sat back in his seat, looking a little perplexed. "No

worries about that."

Aaron hugged David. "You sure?"

Oh . . . cracks were showing. "So, tell us, Jerry. Light bondage sounds kink."

"Well, tying your lover's hands over their hands, blindfolds . . . spreading them out in bed."

"Suspension is better, isn't it?" Troy looked at David. "I mean . . . access to everything . . . ever done it . . . suspended some hot guy . . . played with him for hours . . . fucked him until he couldn't take anymore?"

No one said anything. David was the first to push away from the table. He grabbed the plates. "I'll . . . just start the washing up."

"I'll help you." Troy jumped up and went with him before Aaron could volunteer.

"I'm fine," David said. "I'll ah . . . put things in the dishwasher."

"You've done it, right?" He looked at him. *Yes, damn it, he's done it with me . . . and we weren't alone. Three other hot guys took David . . . while I watched.* It had been the most erotic thing. It had taken Troy months to talk him into it but once he was into it, he'd loved it. "Sometimes a few guys . . . you know . . . I think I'll suggest that to Jerry for his book. Some beautiful guy strung up and played with . . . fucked hard by more than . . ."

"Stop it," David snapped.

Troy looked away, smiled. Guess David did remember. *Missing something in bed, my love?* "I'm sorry. I'm sure it will be quite easy for the two of you to spice it up."

"We don't need spicing up," David said. "It's fine. I'd appreciate it if you'd tone down the sex talk at the table. Okay?"

"I'm sorry. Damn, I'm such an ass. I just thought because Jerry was a writer of erotic fiction . . ."

"Look, I appreciate that," David said. "I appreciate you trying to entertain the guests. Just . . . ah . . . there's a place for everything."

My proper David.

"Thanks for your help today, Randy."

"I want to stay," Troy told him. "I'll stay and help Aaron."
David looked at him.

"I know I don't know you guys well, but I think I should
tell you. I sense something wrong . . . something wrong with
Aaron."

"Nothing's wrong with Aaron." David shook his head.

"Okay." Troy busied himself with the dishes, but he knew
David was looking at him curiously. Okay, he'd planted the
seed. Troy left an hour later, after Aaron told him point blank
he didn't need his help anymore.

"Genesis will be back."

"I hope so," Troy said, and hugged him. "It will be all right,
Aaron," he said softly. "Try not to worry so much, be so
tense."

"I'm not . . . tense," he told Troy.

"Sorry, my mistake." He said goodbye to Jerry and the
writer blew him a kiss.

As Troy walked outside, the writer ran up to him. "Want
to take a walk later?"

"Sure." Troy shrugged. "You could come back to my place
for a drink if you like. Actually, I'd love to talk to you about
Aaron and David."

"Well, I don't know them very well so . . . I'd rather not."

"I think they may be in a sexual slump. Maybe you can
help."

"I can't." He seemed embarrassed. "Not my place to . . . I'm
just a writer."

He was going to be of no use. "Well then," Troy said. "Talk
later, just-a-writer." He slapped the writer's hand and headed
off home.

The next few days Troy jogged with David just to get his
fix of eye-candy so he had fresh jacking off material, but kept

his distance from Typhoon Aaron. Troy figured when Genesis didn't return, sooner or later, brother would come a calling. He did, especially since the husband had gone away with one of his clients for a week.

"I hate to ask you." Aaron sat in front of Troy's house on the beach with him a few days later. "Just didn't expect extra guests. And never expected Rod and Wendy to extend their stay."

Troy was pissed that David had left and hadn't even told him he was going.

"Does he leave you often?" Troy asked.

"It's his job." Aaron shrugged. "He has to go on the road with celebs and stuff sometimes."

"Man or woman?"

"What?"

"Is he gone with a man or woman?"

"It's a man, a movie producer actually."

"Um." Troy looked at him.

"David isn't like that. Were you this suspicious with your ex?"

"My ex fucked around on me all the time. He was a loser. Dave is no loser, but all men are like that when they're away."

"I'm not."

"Yeah, but you've got David in your bed."

Aaron seemed to be trying to figure out what Troy was getting at. Troy didn't give him time to think too much.

"So, how's your sex life? Really?"

"I don't feel comfortable talking to you about that."

"Just tell me, did he fuck you before he left?"

Aaron made a face. "We didn't have time."

"Oh. Um. When he does fuck you, is it good?"

Aaron shook his head and laughed. "Not telling you. Stop it."

"Do you ever fuck him?"

"Sometimes," he said softly.

That pissed Troy off. "But he fucks you mostly?"

"Yeah. He's not . . . a . . . well . . . he can be a bottom but . . . he's mostly a top."

"Does that frustrate you?"

"No," Troy snapped. "Why are we still talking about this? So . . . listen, I'm going to pay you well for pitching in."

"No problem," Troy said, putting a hand on his shoulder. "One thing, do you think it would be better if I actually stayed there, given how early some guests like their breakfast?"

"Sure, that's a good idea. Just until Dave gets back."

"Of course," Troy smiled. "Any news from Genesis?"

"No. I contacted the police."

"Police?" Troy looked at him. "What for? She's an adult."

"She's missing." Aaron got to his feet.

Troy followed. "Probably took off with some guy. You know, Aaron, you look tired."

"I didn't sleep well."

"How come? Another nightmare?"

"Yeah. This one was bad."

He watched the tide come in. "About what?"

"Long story." Aaron shook his head. "We need to plan a menu."

"Great. Let's do it, buddy!"

The following few days were fucked up. *His* David was gone, and Troy was stuck with Aaron, whining about his lack of sleep and how he missed *his* husband. Troy wanted to pound his face to a pulp. *I can't wait to fucking get rid of your sorry ass.*

Aside from that, Troy made himself indispensable to his poor twin, who was overwhelmed by the sudden onslaught of boring, priggish guests. Troy cooked, he cleaned, even supplied aspirin when Aaron complained of headaches. The only time Troy saw Aaron happy was when David called him from Amsterdam.

"He's coming home," he told Troy after one particularly good dinner of roast duckling. "Only thing is, damn it, I won't be here to greet him. He'll be on his way back here when I take off to drive the guests to the airport."

"I'll drive the guests back to the airport tomorrow, so you can be here when he arrives," Troy offered.

"No, I can't impose on you like that. You've done enough. Randy, I couldn't have done this without you."

Troy smiled. "Okay, fine. I'll be here to greet David. I'm going to make a wonderful welcome home breakfast for both of you."

Aaron clapped his hands together. "Perfect."

"How about I set it up in the bedroom as a surprise and leave the rest to you. I'll even take the one last guest out on the boat today to give you guys some snuggle time."

Aaron hugged him. How about that? Troy planned the menu in his mind that evening while Aaron sat watching some music show. He was anticipating his beautiful husband's homecoming.

That night after Aaron went to bed, Troy took the limo for a drive, the one Aaron would use to transport the guests back to the airport in the morning. He made some minor modifications to the gas tank. *Nothing like a slow leak to leave you stranded somewhere for a few hours.*

Troy watched the next morning as Aaron piled the passengers into the limousine and took off. He waved and smiled and went back inside. David was already on his way here. His client had transported him by private plane and the chauffeur would drive him home. What a life.

When another limousine drove up, David got out. The driver handed him his bag and David came walking up the front path. Troy opened the door. "Randy?" he said. "Where's Aaron?"

"Let me take your bag," Troy offered. *Fuck Aaron!*

David handed the bag to Troy.

"I offered to take the guests to the airport, but he insisted. I don't get it." He shook his head. "It was like he wasn't happy you were coming home."

David just stared at him.

"Anyway, he'll be home soon. I'm sure he's just over-worked. I made us breakfast."

"Great," David said. "I'm starved. No word on Genesis?"

"Nothing." Troy shook his head. "Look, it's a little weird but I'd planned a romantic breakfast for both of you, and I set up a table in your bedroom. I'm sorry."

"Does Aaron know?"

"I told him this morning, but he insisted on driving the van. I don't understand it. If you were mine . . ." He paused, smiled. "So, we eat upstairs. It's ready."

David didn't look keen. Troy took his hand and pulled him upstairs. "We can't waste it."

"Randy," David said, stopping outside the bedroom door. "I don't think I want to do this. This feels wrong. What's going on here?"

"Just like I said." Troy opened the door. "Look, see the little table. French toast. You love that."

"Let's take it downstairs." David lifted the entire table and carried it downstairs.

Damn. "You're right of course," Troy said, as he poured them some coffee. He served French toast and all the things he knew David loved to eat. No bacon. David never ate bacon, although he loved the smell. They sat opposite from one another.

"Maybe we can swim later?" Troy suggested.

"Aaron will be home. I'll see what he wants to do. French toast is great."

"You have one guest left. He's a loner, sleeps late. Wanted someone to take him fishing later. You want to join me?"

"Again, let's wait for Aaron."

They finished the breakfast in polite conversation. Troy was a little steamed at David's ingratitude. David spoke about Amsterdam where he went with the producer and Troy did up the dishes. The time passed and David began to check his watch. "I'm going to give Aaron a call on his cell phone."

"Good idea," Troy said, taking Aaron's phone out of his pocket. Thankfully it was off. He put it on the counter then said, "Oh look, David, Aaron's phone. He must have forgotten it." Troy had made sure Aaron couldn't find it this morning.

"Damn it," David said. "I should go looking for him. Maybe the vehicle broke down."

Troy walked over and took his arm. "I doubt it. He'll be back soon. The guest is up. I'll get him some food then take him out. Wish you'd join us."

David jangled his keys. "I'm going after him. Be back soon. And Randy, thanks for holding down the fort."

Troy smiled and watched him leave. It was worth it, worth every minute to have the chance to be a normal couple, to serve David breakfast. Troy was looking forward to doing that full time. Soon, very soon.

CHAPTER FOUR

For a supposedly religious man, Rod let loose a ton of verbal abuse at his maker when they became stranded on the highway to the airport in Lihue. It was only a thirty-one-mile drive but often took close to an hour because of the winding, twisting road and the often inclement weather. Aaron couldn't believe they'd seemed to run out of gas. It was impossible. He'd filled the tank himself the day before and hadn't driven anywhere since.

Why did he get the weird feeling Randy had sabotaged the vehicle? He felt bad even thinking it, but the guy was a real freak. Talking about sex and bondage at the breakfast table. Even the romance writer had seemed a little shocked.

Dave had had a really strange reaction to it. Maybe he's starting to see that Randy is a bit of a headcase.

"Fuck you!" Rod screamed, shaking his fist at the sky. Aaron was trying to figure out why he was so mad at God. Where did he have to get to in such a hurry, anyway?

He lamented that this batch of guests had to fly out of Lihue and not Princeville, which was a lot closer. He sighed and forced himself to remain calm as he called AAA from Wendy's cell phone. Nikko's cell phone battery had met an unfortunate fate in a waterfall, and he was grumpy in the back of the vehicle.

"I mighta missed some important calls," he'd said more than once. He wasn't himself at all. "I can't miss my plane too!" As Aaron waited for an operator, he tried to reassure his passengers that he'd get them to the airport in time for their flights. The AAA dispatch had told him she'd have help on its way within thirty minutes. That was twenty minutes ago. He stood against the car, watching the last of an unexpected downpour dribble away. The ocean was rough, the white peaks dancing atop the churning waves. He couldn't help thinking of Genesis. She might be a hippie, but it wasn't like her not to show up for work. He would drop by her little beach shack today. He'd put it off up until now because he knew she treasured her privacy, but he knew now something was very wrong. She was in trouble. He was certain of it.

He checked his cell phone to make sure he had a signal. The AAA operator had said she'd call him when the mechanic was on his way. He heard a car honking and was astonished to see a woman pulling up behind him, waving madly. He squinted and realized it was Alice, the realtor. He waved back.

Thank God. Maybe she can give the guests a ride to the airport.

She got out of her car, her spiky heels sticking into the wet, red earth. He went right over to her and helped her.

"Is everything okay?" she asked, pushing back a strand of hair from her face.

"Out of gas. No idea how," he said. "But I'm in trouble. I have four guests who need to get to Lihue."

Rod ran over to them. "I have an audition in Honolulu at two o'clock!" he shrieked. "I can't miss it!"

"An audition for what?" Aaron asked. This was news to him.

"*America's Most Wanted.*" He shook his head. "I mean, *American Idol.*"

Aaron almost laughed out loud. "Well, we can't let you miss that."

"I can take you," Alice said. She peered into Aaron's vehicle. "I can squeeze everybody in. I don't have a whole lot of trunk space for luggage, but we'll make do."

"God bless you," Aaron said. He ran to his car and helped

everybody squeeze into Alice's smaller BMW.

"Don't mention his name again," Nikko muttered. "If I hear him mentioned one more time, I'm gonna murder that Jesus freak." He piled into Alice's car and sat, rigid, eyes closed, as though he wished he were anywhere but there.

"Is it true Genesis vanished?" she asked Aaron, as he lugged suitcases out of the trunk. He froze.

"Yes. What have you heard?"

"Only that she hasn't turned up at the coffee shop where she plays, and she hasn't been home. The neighbors heard her dog and cat crying. They took them in, but it doesn't make sense. I heard that you, the neighbors, and Joe who owns the cafe, all contacted the cops, but they have nothing. Not a single lead."

I see the coconut wire is alive and thriving . . ."No, it doesn't make sense, does it?" He felt terrible now that he hadn't gone to her home to check on her. He crammed the bags into Alice's trunk.

"I heard something I can't quite verify. Her neighbors say there was unusual activity at her house yesterday."

"Unusual activity? What's that supposed to mean?" Aaron hated gossip and the islanders were all too keen on it.

"You know she has a son?"

"Yes, I know she does." He didn't say anything else. Genesis had told him this in confidence.

"Well, he's thirteen and goes to school on the mainland. Her ex-husband was getting ready to send him to her for the summer. Guess he won't be now." She waited for a response, but when she got none, she lowered her voice. "She was ex-military. Did you know that?"

Aaron stopped trying to make Wendy's Gucci suitcase fit into the trunk. He hadn't known that about Genesis. It must have showed on his face.

"She walked away from it with an honorable discharge and

a huge pension. I heard some military personnel from Kaneohe Marine Base showed up at her house yesterday."

Aaron was shocked. For Kaneohe to become involved meant that something really terrible must have happened to Genesis . . . or, she had been such a mucky-muck in the military that they'd chosen to become involved.

She straightened when Aaron stopped responding and resumed squeezing suitcases into the tight area.

Alice changed course. "Say, what are you doing about a chef?"

Aaron couldn't stop his grimace. "Our new neighbor pitched in but honestly, it's not really working out."

Alice frowned. "Did his husband ever arrive?"

"*Husband*?" Aaron was shocked.

She spread her hands. "He told my friend at the Halekulani . . ." She turned beet red. "I wasn't gossiping, honest."

"No, no. I'm sure it was business. I know you refer clients there all the time."

"Exactly! Well, she's the desk clerk and also helps with event planning and she asked me if I thought they were serious about getting married there. She wanted to get his contact information to offer them a package deal."

Aaron stared at her, stunned. "I don't think there's a husband. He told me and Dave he got out of a bad relationship," Aaron muttered.

"Oh, dear! Well . . ." She looked flustered. "Perhaps I'm wrong."

Aaron looked at her. They both knew she wasn't. He tactfully moved back to the subject of a chef for Pineapple Hill. "Do you know anyone looking for work as a cook?"

She snapped her fingers. "As a matter of fact, I do. Nice guy. Name is Franklin Reynolds. He's been working in Maui but just got laid off from his job as a short-order cook at the Maui Grand breakfast bar. Apparently, they're doing away

64

with it. He's been wanting something a bit more laid back. His sister, Lani, who owns the Heliconia Inn, is a very good friend of mine. She mentioned it to me in an email. He's a mad surfer, so I think your place is perfect."

"He sounds like a good fit." Aaron liked the idea of another guy around the premises. A kind of buffer between him and pesky Randy Carlton.

When did he become such an intrusive fixture in our lives?

Aaron didn't have much contact with other hoteliers except the B and B owners. He knew the Heliconia Inn was a private hotel on the far slopes of a golf course. "Do you think it's all right for me to call her?"

"I can do better than that." She began fixing her Bluetooth over her ear. I'll call her right now. I'll have her call your cell."

"Great. Oh, wait. I left my cell phone at home. Wendy let me borrow hers. Please tell Lani I'll call her the moment I get home. We owe you big time." Aaron slammed her trunk shut.

"Anything for a friend." She beamed at him. She suddenly laid a hand on his arm. "I hope you don't think I'm callous trying to fill Genesis' position so quickly."

"No, I hope you don't think I am."

She shook her head. "Business is business."

He gave her a quick hug and bid farewell to his guests.

"I'll never forget this trip!" one guest called out to him. "I'll stay in touch."

"Please do." Aaron stepped away from the car and felt a moment of panic stuck out here without a cell phone. He hadn't even had a chance to call David and let him know he was stuck.

"If you're still here when I come back from picking up my new client at Lihue Airport, I'm taking you home with me," Alice said.

"Okay, thanks." He waved as she peeled away, the others waving back. He was worried that he wouldn't get all his chores done in time for the new arrivals.

A few seconds later, he heard a familiar honk. His heart leapt in his chest.

"Dave!" he called out, never happier to see his handsome husband.

"What happened?" Dave got out of his car, anxiety etched onto his features.

"Ran out of gas."

"You forgot to fill it?"

"That's just it. I filled it last night."

Dave frowned and began poking under the hood.

"Triple A's coming," Aaron said.

"How'd you manage that? You left your cell phone at home." Dave came away from the hood, reached into his back pocket and handed it to Aaron.

"Oh, baby, thank you. I borrowed Wendy's. What did we ever do without these things?" His cell phone rang. An 808 number. Somebody in the islands. He took the call. It turned out to be Lani, the hotelier. Aaron talked to her briefly, then explained to Dave about Franklin.

"That's an excellent idea." Dave glanced up at him. "You didn't run out of gas. This thing's got a leak."

Aaron resumed his conversation. Lani told him Franklin would be out on the first available flight that afternoon. "You're really helping him," she said. "He's just gone through a bad divorce and now this."

Bad relationships seemed to be catching. He ended the call just as the Triple A arrived. He and Dave went over the car and muttered to one another.

"This kind of leak is unusual and expensive to fix," the mechanic told them. "I'd say somebody did this deliberately. Kids, most probably. All bored out of their minds around here. All got rock fever."

Aaron and Dave exchanged glances. They didn't know any kids and very few ever came to this side of the island for vacations with their parents for that very reason. It was a paradise for those seeking rest. Not Disneyland and McDonalds. The kids who did come usually stayed at one of the big, splashy, all-inclusive hotels that offered canoeing and surfing lessons, three meals a day, and nonstop resort activities.

A long, long way away from Pineapple Hill.

They let the driver tow the vehicle all the way into Lihue to their own mechanic. Dave called the mechanic who said he'd check out the leak and let them know his prognosis.

"Need a ride, handsome?" Dave cracked to Aaron.

"Yeah. If I get to babysit your cock."

Dave grinned. "And Randy said you weren't pleased that I was coming home."

"What!"

Dave waved his hand. "I'm beginning to think he's a bit of a nutter. Harmless, but not quite all there. I couldn't believe he started talking about whips and chains over breakfast. That'd look awkward on TripAdvisor, wouldn't it?"

Aaron threw himself into Dave's arms. "You know I couldn't wait for you to get back here, right?"

Dave smiled. "Show me."

"I will." Aaron got into the car beside him, but as much as he wanted to show Dave how much he'd missed him, he agonized over the destruction Randy was causing in their lives.

"Did you know that Randy told the hotel clerk at the Halekulani that he was coming here to meet his husband and that he was thinking of getting married there?"

"Can't be. He told us he was getting over a bad breakup."

"I know, I know. Alice is stumped, too." Aaron repeated his conversation with Alice.

"Huh." Dave slumped back in his seat. "What the hell is this guy up to?"

"I don't know." Aaron didn't want to give Randy any more room in their lives. The guy had inserted himself way too far, way too soon.

Not any longer. Dave's a soft touch but I'm not going to be so nice. I'm taking my power back. Wow. Why am I thinking this way? It's the way I used to feel when . . .

When Troy was alive.

"Are you okay?" Dave asked.

"Very." Aaron gave him a seductive smile, trying not to think about how stung he'd felt with Randy when he had made rude remarks about how lucky Aaron was that Dave wanted a man like him and obviously he didn't have much experience.

He closed his eyes and kissed Dave, enjoying the way their roadside hug began to turn so sensual. He broke off their embrace.

"When I was a teenager I fantasized about other boys. I used to watch some of the scouts in my group pretend they were doing uphill sprints, but they'd split off and one day I caught two of them behind this old shack that was our base. They were on the ground, their uniforms in disarray . . ."

Dave was watching, listening to him, captivated by this tale.

Aaron began to fumble in his man's pants and took hold of David's smooth, luscious cock. "I watched them giving each other fast and thirsty head. I never heard sounds like that before. The pleasure they sought and gave. They'd pretend to hate each other in front of everyone else but they secretly needed one another's cocks. I need to suck *your* cock, Dave. And you need to pretend you're keeping an eye out for our scout master."

He gasped as Aaron's hands galloped to his zipper to release more of his thick cock to his mouth. Aaron kissed and licked its length. He could sense Dave's frustration until he found his way into Aaron's mouth again.

Dave stroked his hair as he sucked at him. "Don't know what's gotten into you lately, babe, but you're on fire these days."

Aaron began to rub his two index fingers against one another as he sucked up and down the shaft. Then he added his thumbs. It took some dexterity to remember to rub his fingers in opposite directions against the slick shaft, as well as keeping a tight hold on the head with his lips, but he managed it.

"That feels . . ." Dave moaned, gasped, gripped the door handle, slapped the roof.

I feel a monster orgasm coming. Damn, that porno scene I watched really works!

"Oh, fuck!" Dave screamed. "Oh . . . man . . ."

The friction of the opposing finger strokes sent him over the edge faster than Aaron had expected. Dave gripped his head and his cock tore down Aaron's throat. He came, his whole body shaking. Aaron glanced down. Even his feet were trembling.

I feel like a pro! Take that, Randy. Yeah. A man like me knows how to give some rockin' head!

Dave's chest heaved until he finally caught his breath. He couldn't lift his head from the seat rest. "You have such a nasty streak in you, baby."

"You brought it out." He leaned over and kissed Dave.

"Aaron, this island sun . . . or maybe it's the red dirt, is bringing out a dangerous side, the bad boy in you."

"Is that good?"

He grinned at me. "Oh, it's amazing. You just blew my mind."

Back at the bed and breakfast, Aaron was furious when he saw the breakfast tray Randy had prepared, allegedly for the two of them. Dave told Aaron that Randy had tried to persuade him to share it with him.

"I came to find you instead," Dave said.

It irked Aaron that Randy had made such a fantastic

breakfast for Dave, but slapped stuff together for their guests. Randy took so long with even basic menu items, Aaron tried hard not to urge him to move faster.

No. That short-order cook couldn't get here quick enough.

He was pleased when Franklin Reynolds called him, as Aaron and Dave worked to clean the two rental cottages and the house rooms in preparation for their guests. The truth was, Aaron usually enjoyed getting ready for new guests. He loved people and taking care of them, but not all of their guests were wonderful. That was the beauty of having a high-end, boutique property. If you really didn't warm to somebody, they would be gone in a matter of days and other, interesting people soon turned up.

Franklin seemed excited about the prospect of spending time in Kauai. Aaron assured him they would give him a staff room. They had two very small cottages reserved for this very purpose. Each had a bed, bathroom, and tiny kitchenette, but staff had kitchen privileges in the house.

"I'm flying in on the six-thirty go! Airlines flight," Franklin said. "I look forward to discussing the breakfast menu with you and anything else you need me to help you with."

"I do, too," Aaron said. "I'll pick you up—"

"No, no. I'm renting a car. I like to surf on the Na'Pali coast, so I need a vehicle. I'm shipping my own to me, but it won't arrive until the weekend."

"Very good." He sounded solid and self-sufficient.

As he ended the call, Dave came running to him. "Code cracker!"

"What?" Aaron asked.

"Our Genesis. She was a CIA code cracker! She apparently was captured in some Middle-East country six years ago and was tortured. Held prisoner for seventy-nine days. She never gave up a thing and broke out of there, rescuing three of her staff in the process. Apparently whatever drugs they gave her fried her brain."

"Oh, my God!"

"I know, right?" Dave ran a hand through his hair. "The government isn't going to let this thing die down. They consider her a precious gem. They say they don't understand why she would disappear. They think she's been murdered. They're about to launch a search for her."

"Where did you hear all this?" Aaron asked, as the whir of choppers pierced the silence.

"On the news! It's on TV and all over the Internet. And, I just got a call. There is some field sergeant coming over to ask us questions."

Aaron stared at Dave. He wanted the authorities to find Genesis, but what if they began nosing around their bed and breakfast thinking they'd had something to do with it?

And what about their new arrivals? How would they feel about the investigation when all they wanted was peace and quiet? He could barely think with the noise of the choppers now.

Aaron's cell phone rang. It was Annie, his friend in Princeville who ran a Bed and Breakfast establishment there.

"Hello, toots," she said. "Geez, what's all that noise?"

"Helicopters. Police helicopters."

"Really? My God! Just because of some bed bugs?"

"What are you talking about?" Aaron struggled to not only hear her but to make sense of her conversation.

"Bed bugs," she repeated. "It's all over the Internet."

"Bed bugs are all over the Internet?"

"*Your* bed bugs," she corrected.

"*My* bed bugs?"

"What's going on?" Dave demanded.

"You mean you really don't know?" Annie asked.

"Annie, for God's sake. What are you talking about?" Aaron snapped.

"Somebody's just posted two scathing reviews about Pineapple Hill on Yelp and TripAdvisor. Whoever it is also tweeted people to avoid the place. As a matter of fact, Alice was the one who told me."

Aaron repeated all this to Dave.

"The thing is," Annie soothed, "there are no bed bugs in Kauai. Waikiki, yes. And as you know from our last bulletin, some were found in a small hotel in Puna on the Big Island. But the hotel guest who found them alerted the owners. They didn't blast it all over Facebook."

Aaron began to sway out of total fear. "It's on Facebook?"

"Whoever posted this did it to cause you harm, but I think you should know, you might get the county health inspector showing up for a spot check."

Aaron repeated this to Dave as well.

"What do we do?" Aaron asked her.

"Check everything," she urged. "We're all behind you. We know your place is clean. Check all the places bed bugs like to hide. Who knows? Maybe somebody brought them in unknowingly in their suitcase?"

"I can't believe this is happening." Aaron felt like his life was falling apart. Dave was on his knees on the living room floor screaming at the TripAdvisor review.

"Listen to this," he read aloud. "This is the worst of the worst. I'd rather stay in a rat hole of a Mexican jail than spend a single hour at Pineapple Hill." He looked up at Aaron. "Who the hell could have written this?"

Aaron shook his head. "You think it was Steve and Eileen?"

"Retaliation for the dispute over the trashed room?" Dave went silent. "Maybe," he said finally, "but that was weeks ago, and we never charged their credit card. We didn't push it. Usually angry people fire off a review right away. This has to be somebody else."

Aaron's cell phone rang. It was the concierge at the Moana Surfrider Hotel in Honolulu. He couldn't believe how swiftly news of the alleged bed bugs had traveled. He had a couple booked into one of the cottages who'd just read the reviews and wanted to cancel.

"I tried to explain to them that there are no bed bugs in Kauai." The man sounded worried. "It isn't true, is it?"

"No, of course it isn't true. We believe it was a fake review but have no idea who wrote it. I can assure you we have no bed bugs." Aaron hoped he sounded confident.

"Well, they are reluctant to chance it. Would you be willing to let them come at a reduced rate?"

Aaron couldn't believe it. "They are willing to chance it for a discount?" He forced himself to chuckle. "No, I'm sorry. They booked this trip weeks ago, and they are supposed to be arriving today. It's too late, per our contract, for them to receive a refund and I don't see why we should give them a reduced rate for no reason."

"A bad review. Bed bugs," the concierge said.

"Bad reviews happen. And we have no bed bugs." Aaron caught Dave's eye and was relieved to see his husband supporting his stance. "Please let me know what they decide," Aaron said and ended the call.

"We need to bring in a pest control company pronto. We need proof we're bug free, then I'm going to post a response on both the review sites."

"Don't forget Facebook."

Dave looked mad. "This is disgusting. Why the hell did somebody do this?" Dave was staring at him now.

"Don't look at me," Aaron said. "I have no idea." He hated the look of uncertainty on his husband's face. After Googling for signs of bed bugs, Aaron went through all the rooms. He checked the mattresses, pulling up all the bedding. He checked under the cushions of the sofas. What worried him was that every single resource he read mentioned bed bugs were notoriously hard to beat.

He found nothing but kept itching. It was psychosomatic, he knew, but he was a bundle of nerves now and those nerves weren't going to ease up any time soon.

I just had to go and open a Bed and Breakfast . . .

Dave called a local pest control outfit. The father and son arrived in minutes. Aaron and Dave had been grateful at their speed until it transpired they'd been watching the news.

"This is where the lady spy works, eh?" the father asked.

Aaron grimaced. "She's not a spy. She was our chef, and our friend. Can you please come this way?" He led the two men to the cottages and then through the rooms. They also checked the main house and the staff cottages. They seemed disappointed not to have found bed bugs but did report a brown recluse spider in Aaron's private office.

"A brown recluse?" Aaron was stunned. "But they're deadly, aren't they? I didn't even know they existed."

"Well, we do get them in Hawaii, but not around these parts much," came the response. The two men killed the spider and treated the window frame it had been lurking in.

"How did it get there?" he kept asking them. They had no idea. They wrote up their invoice and put in writing that there were no bed bugs in Pineapple Hill and charged Aaron and Dave a small fortune for their emergency appointment.

"They didn't mention it was an emergency charge," Dave grumbled when they left, "but at least we have it in writing that we have no goddamned bed bugs." He wrote his response on the websites as Aaron called the health department and asked the kind lady on the other end of the phone if he needed to fax the inspection report to her.

"For bed bugs?" she asked. "We don't have any in Hawaii."

"I know. We got a fake review." He tried to explain things and she finally seemed to get it.

"Some people need to get a life," she fumed. "We've never had a single complaint about your property, Mr. Alvarez. Why don't you go ahead and scan that form and send it to me, please?" She gave him her email address. He was now petrified to go into his office in case the spider had brought some buddies to jump out at him as he worked at his desk.

He had to do it though and braced himself. To his dismay, however, people were cancelling their long-term travel arrangements and a lot of his B and B owner friends were worried that something was really wrong.

Aaron had no time to deal with it all. They expected new arrivals any time now. The concierge from the Moana called back and said, "We believe your establishment is not only unsanitary, but it now the subject of a police investigation. Either cancel the reservation without any charge or you will never receive a recommendation from us again. Ever."

He had no choice. He relieved his clients of their obligation to Pineapple Hill. He could have wept when he looked at his schedule. Sixteen cancellations in twenty minutes.

The Internet was indeed a wonderful, yet terrible, thing.

Outside he could hear the whine of the choppers in the distance.

Good. The farther, the better . . .

He heard a car out front and got up from his desk. He had to remind himself to pick up a fresh flower lei from the fridge. It was the last one. But he'd bought a batch of new ones yesterday . . . hadn't he? Confused he went outside, stunned to see a police vehicle and some sort of official state vehicle with the US and Hawaiian flags on the front.

"Mr. Alvarez? David Alvarez?" the first man asked.

"No. I'm Aaron Alvarez. David's inside."

Dave came out, putting his arm around Aaron. "Is this about Genesis?" he asked.

"May we come inside?" the first man asked.

"Of course," Aaron said, trying to be the polite host, but his gaze fell on the unlikely sight of Alice walking along the beach right outside their property. She was crying as she talked animatedly to an angry-looking Randy Carlton . . .

Chapter Five

Alice was getting carried away, and personally it was time to end it. Troy glanced over at the official looking car in from of the B and B and sucked in some breath. He'd heard the news reports, of course, but there was nothing for him to worry about, nothing to tie him to Genesis' disappearance.

"I'm sorry," Alice said, wiping her eyes. "I didn't know how important this job was to you. I thought you were a model."

"I *am* a model." He sighed, reaching over and giving her a pat. "Dry your eyes now. It's just that I . . . well . . . helping those boys," he looked over at Aaron, who was looking over to where they stood, "has become a quest. I'm going to tell you something I've told no one, a confession Aaron told me the other night."

Alice drew closer. "What is it?"

Yes, bitch, you really need to know. Gossips were so convenient. He lowered his voice. "Aaron told me he gets so lonely when David leaves him . . . and sometimes . . . only occasionally, he's slept with a guest or two."

Alice put a hand to her mouth and stared over at Aaron and David, who were engaged in conversation with the official looking men. "Poor David, oh my God. Are you sure he doesn't know?"

"No, and don't you tell him," Troy snapped. "Listen, Aaron loves David. He told me if he ever lost him, he'd drown himself. He has dreams about drowning . . . about a boat and . . . his twin who died . . ."

"He had a twin?" Alice whispered.

Troy nodded. "Yes. Actually, I heard . . . don't quote me, that Aaron had something to do with his twin's death . . . that he wanted David. David was married at one time to Aaron's brother."

"Holy . . . Goodness!" Alice gasped.

"Okay, so Aaron needs me. Can't you do something about that Franklin guy?"

"May not need him now that they have bed bugs."

"They don't have bed bugs." Troy shook his head. "It's impossible. I can't believe some people saying that!" But the Internet was a wonderful thing to get the word out about stuff. "So, how about you let Franklin know there's trouble here . . . so he doesn't want the job. Listen, now with the police all over and . . ."

The two men in suits were heading in their direction. Troy smiled as they approached. "We'll talk about it later, Alice," he said.

"You've been a good friend to them."

"I don't want to see David heartbroken because Aaron can't keep it in his . . ." He trailed off and held out his hand to the men. "Hello, sirs."

The first man, tall and lean with grey hair, took his hand. The other nodded at him. "Randy Carlton?" The first one checked his pad. "I'm told you just bought a house down the beach?"

"Yes," he said. "Pretty nice place."

He turned to Alice and she introduced herself. "You sold Mr. Carlton the house," he said.

"Yes." She handed the man her card. "If you're ever in need."

"Thank you," he muttered, tucking the card in his pocket. "Did you both know Genesis Pratt?"

"I did," Troy said. "Not well but she was working for my

neighbours when I first met them a month or so ago. She was a little spacey . . . smoked pot . . . sat on the beach . . . sometimes slept there."

"When was the last time you saw her?" The man asked.

"Oh . . . um . . . let's see. Saw her one night on my way home, about two weeks ago. I told her she shouldn't be out there alone late at night."

"How late was it?"

"Midnight, maybe," Troy said. "She was drinking. I saw a bottle in her hand."

"Drinking what?" The man asked him, jotting it down.

"I don't know. I wasn't close enough. I was on my way home. I just waved, called out from a distance, and kept going."

"And you," the man turned to Alice. "Did you know her?"

"Not well. I saw her on the beach sometimes . . . like Randy did. She wandered quite a bit, slept outside occasionally. She was a good cook. She made me breakfast once. That's about it. She was a very quiet person."

"Okay." The two men looked at each other. "You've been very helpful."

"I hope you find her," Troy said.

"So do we," the man replied and followed the other back to the vehicle.

Troy looked at Alice. "You should phone that cook. No point in him getting involved in all this. He'll only blame you for it and your rep will be shot."

"Oh dear," Alice said, "never thought of that." She took out her cell phone.

"Better get back to the house, see if I can offer some support to Aaron and David. Remember, what I told you about Aaron is confidential . . . and I never said anything about medication and head doctors or anything."

"What?" Alice stared at him.

Troy walked away. He smiled, only sobering again as he got to where Aaron and David sat talking outside on the stoop. "Are you guys all right?" he asked.

Aaron looked up at him. "Fine," he said stiffly.

"Just horrible about Genesis. I hope they find her. I told the cops all I knew."

"What was going on between you and Alice anyway?" Aaron demanded, meeting his gaze.

Nosey little bitch. "What do you mean?"

"She seemed really upset. She was crying," David added.

"Oh, she's a little upset about Genesis. We all are."

"She hardly knew Genesis," Aaron protested.

"I think they knew each other more than ... well ... enough about that." Troy looked down at the sand.

"What?" David asked.

"Well ... I think they were having a ... Alice doesn't want the authorities to know ... doesn't want to be a suspect."

"What do you mean by suspect? What's going on?" Aaron got to his feet.

"I think they were sleeping together." Troy sighed heavily.

"Genesis and Alice?" David gave Troy a look of disbelief. "They had nothing in common."

"Opposites attract." Troy shrugged. "I can't be sure, but I think she was alluding to it. I don't want to get in on gossip. Look at the harm it does. I can't believe the shit on the Internet. Have you had many cancellations?"

David nodded.

"This could ruin us." Aaron looked stricken.

"It won't," Troy said gently. "This stuff passes ... people forget crap. Why not contact all your former guests and ask them to write some positive reviews?"

"That's a great idea." David looked at Aaron.

"I'll do it for you ..." Troy offered, "if you want. I'd have to borrow your computer. I don't have Internet hooked up yet."

Silence.

"Come on," he coaxed.

David was on his side. "Let him," he said to Aaron. "You rest."

"Better yet . . ." Troy grinned. "Why don't you guys go somewhere for a nice, romantic dinner together . . . even get a room in the city? I'll look after this place. I'll clean up and do the computer stuff. It will all seem better when you get back. Okay?"

Aaron actually smiled at Troy. "I . . . that's really nice of you, Randy. I . . ."

"Well then go, before I decide it's too nice." He nudged him.

Aaron looked at David. David nodded.

An hour later, the hotel room was booked, and Aaron and David were on their way to the airport. Troy stood in front of their house, waving them off. He had twenty-four hours and he intended to use every single hour wisely.

He called his agent. "Hello, Mona, darling," he said. "You rang?"

"Randy, you cad!" she chastised him in her nasally tone. "Where have you been, girlfriend? I've left fifty messages. I have a job for you, a swimsuit ad for Men's Beachwear Limited. They want you to model their new 'barely there' swim thong and a host of other beach fashions. Money, money. They're going to meet you at your house. That hunky camera man you've been doing wants to film it there on the island."

"He wants to jump my bones. He's a bit of a stalker, actually."

"Um, yes, but he's hung like a . . . donkey. He looks lost in the seventies . . . long hair, moustache but no complaints . . . killer body. Did you know he was a former model himself?"

"Yes, and he's a whiz with the camera. I'll call him to see

what time he's coming."

"I assume he'll come tonight before the crew."

"Perfect. You coming tomorrow?"

"I wish. I'll send the contracts by courier. Ta, ta. Have fun with Russ."

Troy hung up his cell phone and walked into the small office. He fired up the Internet. Aaron had showed him the contact file for all the former clients before he left that morning and starred the clients who were especially happy with their stay. Troy copied and pasted the emails and asked them to please write a review to counteract the nasty rumours of bedbugs. Within an hour, fifty-two had responded and wrote glowing reviews. Troy sat back with a smile. No sense in punishing David, and someone would be grateful.

Now, his good deed was done, it was time for Aaron's exploits to be revealed. Poor David. Troy hoped he wasn't too upset when he found out what Aaron had been doing behind his back. *No worries. I'll be around to comfort him.*

The phone rang later that afternoon. It was Franklin. "Mr. Alvarez? Aaron?"

"Yes, this is Aaron." They could speak in exactly the same voice.

"I . . . I'm sorry to have to say this but given all that's going on out there, I think I'll pass on the job. I hope it doesn't leave you in a spot."

Troy did a little dance but kept his voice calm. "Well, can't say I'm happy, but it's your choice. Things will calm down. Sure you won't reconsider?"

"No, I don't think so."

"Thanks, Franklin, for letting me know." Troy hung up. "Um," he said aloud, "can't get good help these days."

"Now." He went back to the computer. "Let's take a look at my husband's bank account." Troy went into the bank website where David had always done business. He keyed in all

David's personal information. He knew it by heart. Then he entered his password. Shit. He'd changed it. But he knew David. It would be something familiar. After a few tries, he used his birthday, the same as Aaron's, and added two digits from Dave's licence plate number. *That was it. He was in.*

Troy smiled, sat back. He knew Aaron had access. He heard David tell Aaron to pay the utility bill from his online account. He checked the balance in the savings account. Very nice. David had socked quite a bit away but then his job paid really well, not like this dump.

"Okay, so now let's send all this money to Aaron's account at his bank." Troy took Aaron's bank book out of his pocket. *You should never leave these things just lying around.* Aaron had a measly two grand in his account. Not a saver. *Okay, let's just send one hundred and fifty-two thousand dollars to my dear twin.* "Sooner or later, David, you'll know he's robbed you blind. He's been dishonest with you from the beginning." He waited while the transfer took place then logged out of the account.

Troy took out his cell phone and dialed. It rang three times then picked up. "Randy?"

"Hey, baby. When are you getting here? I can't wait."

"I'm on the plane, babe. Waiting to take off. It won't be long."

"Did you bring me what I asked?"

"It wasn't easy."

"Things should never be too easy in life, Russ. You know that. Your reward is waiting for you."

"Will you model the thong for me?"

"Sure." Troy rolled his eyes. *Fuckin' loser.* "Just make sure they're perfect." Troy hung up.

Two hours later, Russ drove up in a rental car. Troy walked out to meet him. "Anyone see you?"

"Don't think so." He got out of the car. "Give me a kiss."

"Fuck off, Russ. Later," he muttered. "Get inside." Troy pushed him in and closed the door. "Show me."

Russ handed him an envelope and Troy walked over to the counter and took out the glossy photographs. He studied them. "A God damned masterpiece," he grinned at Russ. He could have danced again, he was so happy.

Russ sat down at the counter. "Wasn't easy, posing your brother's face on a naked torso with another body doing the nasty with him, coupled with that pic of the bedroom you sent me."

"It's great. Looks clear enough yet . . . not too clear . . . to see any lines. You are magic. And the letter, did you send that email to both of them?"

"Yep. About an hour ago."

"That should be a damper on their romantic getaway."

"What is this all about anyway, Randy?"

"Just a joke . . . a funny joke."

"Quite sappy, these letters you made me send. All this stuff about how much they loved each other and how Alvarez was waiting for the right moment to rip this David guy off so they could run away together. Is this stuff true? How do you come up with all this stuff, baby?" Russ tried to kiss him.

Troy pushed him away. "I'm a genius. Now forget it."

"So, you promised to model the thong?"

"I will. And I'll fuck you, too, just like I promised."

Russ rubbed his groin.

"But you got to do something for me first."

"Thought I just did?"

"You did. But something else."

"What? I'll do anything for you, baby." Russ pulled him close.

"You're going to beat the hell out of me, but not the face."

Russ released him, narrowed his eyes. "What?"

"You heard me. I'll put on the thong if you beat the hell out of me."

"I'm not going to . . ."

"Yes, baby." Troy stroked his hair. "You are. So come on. Grab me and drag me down to the beach. We'll fuck at my place . . . all night if you want." Troy tongued his ear.

"You want me to . . ."

"Grab me and be rough. I like it. It will turn me on big time."

Russ shrugged. He grabbed his arm and dragged Troy out the door. He stopped to pick up his bag then continued to pull Troy along the sand. Troy hollered and struggled all the way down the beach. Russ tore open the door to his house.

"You want to fuck me then hurt me!" Troy hollered.

Russ pushed him into the house. He threw the thong at him. "Put it on, slut."

"Don't hurt me," Troy pleaded.

Russ smiled. "Oh, I'm going to hurt you, baby! We're playing, right?"

"Right," Troy muttered. *What a moron!*

Russ started to get into it.

Troy took off his clothes and put on the thong. He gave Russ a seductive look. "Come on, hurt me."

Three hours later, Troy sent Russ on his way. He'd given him his fuck and Russ had left him black and blue. Troy picked his cell phone off the nightstand and called Aaron. If he called David, Aaron would go nuts, so better do it this way.

Aaron answered on the third ring. It was dinner time. "Randy? Is everything all right?" he asked.

"Aaron . . ." he moaned. "I'm sorry."

"Randy? Randy, what's wrong?"

"My ex . . . he found me . . . the one who . . . he hurt me, Aaron. He hurt me really good this time."

"Oh my God. Did you call the police?"

"No, no police. He'll come back. He'll kill me." Troy pretended to sob. "I'm so sorry to ruin your trip. I'll go back to the house and lock up. Should be all right . . . aw . . ."

"Randy. You need to go to the hospital."

"No. I'm okay, just some bruises. I want you guys to have some down time. I did the Internet stuff. You've had some great comments. I'm sure business will be fine . . ."

"We haven't checked our Internet. We've made a conscious choice not to. Randy, I want you to . . ."

"I do have some bad news, but it can wait until . . . ooh . . . until you get back."

"What bad news? Randy, do you have a restraining order on that guy?"

"Not yet but I guess . . . I'll have to. Maybe you can go to the police with me when you get back. Aaron," Troy cried, "I value your friendship so much. You've been like a . . . a . . . brother to me."

Silence.

"Aaron?"

"Thanks . . . of course . . . I'll go with you to the police but tell me the bad news?"

"Franklin got scared off by the negative pub."

"Shit."

"I'll do all I can to help you. Where's David? Don't ruin his trip by telling him all this."

"He's gone downstairs to get his sunglasses. He left them at the bar. I think we should come home."

"I'll call Alice, okay?"

"You promise?"

"I will. I promise. Have fun. Don't worry about anything until you get back."

You'll have your hands full, brother. Wait until David realises you've emptied his account and he sees the desperate email and photographs of you and your lover – a guy who'd actually stayed here a year ago writing to say he couldn't wait for you any longer. He never wanted to see you again. And David will need some time to think . . . and I . . . battered by the man I love as well . . . David and I will have everything in common. Then . . . well . . . Aaron, you will be so depressed . . . the man you love won't believe anything you say . . . and suicide will be your only option . . . at least that's what the police report will say.

Aaron had hung up. "Sorry to rain on your parade, Aaron." Troy laughed and hunted down Alice's card. He dialled. "Alice?"

"Randy?"

"I need . . . your help."

"What's wrong?"

"Can you come?" He started to cry. "My ex found me and he's . . . he beat me up."

"My Lord. Is he gone?"

"Yes. Please, I don't want to be alone."

"I'm on my way."

While Troy waited, he took out the pictures of David he'd taken on their honeymoon. He studied them again. They made his cock hard. Then he reached over and opened the other box he kept always on his person. He'd been saving these for a special occasion. It was now time to celebrate. Everything had gone perfectly. Soon David would be his again. Troy withdrew the two photographs. It was a shame Dave hadn't let him keep them all. He'd freaked when David knew he took these. Troy had had to burn most of them in the fireplace but David never found these two. And these were the best.

Troy lay back and started to massage his cock through the thong, his tongue moved around his lips as he focussed on every detail. Three hot and hung young call boys with their hands all over his man. They'd oiled David's skin, stroked his cock until it was hard. Dave's hands caught over his head. He was blindfolded, on his knees on the huge, round bed. One blond head was over Dave's left nipple, one dark head behind him, and another hot boy with a greased dildo in his hand ready to shove it into Dave's beautiful ass. Troy loved this picture. It was foreplay. He felt the pressure build in his cock.

He waited a second then lifted the second picture. As he did, the come rushed through him, and he cried out. My beautiful husband, being used—his ass, his mouth, his cock, and Dave's head was back, a look of pure pleasure on his face while Troy watched it all.

The come dripped through his fingers and he swallowed. He'd sent the callboys home after that. He'd walked over to the bed, and David was there, the blindfold gone, his thighs open. He looked at Troy with such lust, Troy nearly had a heart attack. He rode David's cock that night, looking down into his eyes and Troy was lost, Dave's cock buried deep inside him. David rolled Troy over and hammered him again, practically roaring with ferocious need. His David was so horny he'd fucked Troy four times that night. It was the best sex they'd ever had. Troy wanted that again. He wanted him again soon. Troy wasn't prepared to wait much longer.

When he heard Alice pull up, Troy hid the pictures under his bed and hobbled to the door. He wasn't faking that.

When she saw him, Alice let out a cry. "You poor darling. Oh my God, Randy. You need to go to the hospital."

"No. Here." Troy gave Alice to key to the B and B. "Can you lock up. Russ dragged me out of there and I didn't have time to lock up properly."

"Of course. What else can I do?" Alice looked frantic.

"Come back and be with me. I don't want to be alone tonight."

She left to do his bidding and he sighed. Troy didn't anticipate spending anything but a boring night with Alice but it was worth it. It would probably be his last night without David. He was sure poor David would be bunking on his sofa the next night, crying over Aaron. What did he expect? Aaron had pretended to be his husband initially, anyone who could fake that shit, could fake anything.

Troy called his agent to cancel the photo shoot tomorrow.

He briefly told her what had happened. She was concerned but miffed about the lost contract. Too bad!

Troy lay down on the sofa after he hung up. He almost fell asleep thinking he should take some aspirin. It hurt if he moved around too much but it was superficial. He thought about all the money he'd hidden, about the things David and him would be able to do with it. David loved travelling and now they'd do it together. Troy could picture them making love on the French Riviera, sipping champagne, David naked . . . a couple of sweet young guys sucking on his nipples, playing with Dave's cock, getting it ready just for Troy. And he'd wear this thong. It would drive David wild. And he'd never let the boys get fucked by David, although they were frothing at the mouths to have his cock up their asses. No . . . that cock went only in his ass . . . ever.

Alice was back. She brought him a blanket, probably turned on by the thong. "Sorry, Russ made me pose for him in that."

"Oh. Do you still love this guy?" she asked, sitting on a chair. "Is this the husband you spoke of on the mainland?"

"Husband? Oh . . . no," Troy said. "I was married. Some guy stole him from me. He was good to me, Alice. So handsome. He would never hurt me. He loved me so much, but I screwed it up. We're talking now. He misses me. The guy he is with . . . well . . . he's cheating on him . . . robbing him blind."

"That's terrible."

"Yes, but I think it's going to happen, us being back together. It was meant to be, Alice."

"Aww," she said, smiling.

"I think he's going to see that guy for what he is . . . and come back to me. It's a matter of time."

"Does your husband know this Russ guy?"

"No. It was a mistake on my part, but he's obsessed with

me. Listen, I don't want to talk about him. You hungry?"

"Yeah, a little."

"Why don't you make us a sandwich? I managed to do some food shopping."

"Sounds great." She got up and went to the kitchen. "You want coffee?"

"Sure."

Later they sat eating their sandwiches and Alice put him to sleep with talk about abuse counselling. He assured her it was over and dozed off. When he woke up in the morning, Alice was gone. She left a note. "Gone to work. If you need me, call me."

"I won't be needing you," Troy muttered, squished up the note and threw it across the room. His cell phone rang. He answered it. "Russ?"

"Are you all right? I worried about you all night. I didn't want to do that to you. Randy, I love you. Baby. Please tell me you're all right?"

"Russ, never fuckin' call me again. You hear me? If you do, I'll have you arrested for assault. You got your money. You served your purpose. I'm madly and passionately in love with someone else. We'll be together soon, so I don't ever want to see you again. You understand? Come near me, and I'll kill you." He put the phone down then went to get some aspirin.

He checked the time. It was after ten. They'd be home soon, another few hours, and everything would come together like a beautiful symphony. He made some coffee and went to look in the mirror. The bruises on his arms and legs and ribcage were purple. He grinned through the pain and sipped his coffee. He pulled on some shorts and a t-shirt and walked outside. He looked down the beach to see some vehicles, ambulance, coroner, and police. "Looks like they found poor Genesis." He shook his head and clicked his tongue. "Tide must have swept her in. Just proves you shouldn't drink on the beach in the dark." He sighed. "More misery for my poor twin, well . . . c'est la vie!" And immediately Troy began humming that tune.

CHAPTER SIX

It was a nightmare. Aaron was not the one who'd suggested a night at the hotel. *He* was not the one who created all of this.

Randy was. And now he was nowhere to be found.

He was an instigator. That's what he was. In the space of less than twenty-four hours, Aaron's life was in ruins. For the second time that morning, Dave got off the phone and turned to Aaron, his face twisted with rage.

"The bank says the money was transferred to my account yesterday." He squared his shoulders and gripped Aaron's office desk. He'd commandeered it the moment he'd checked his cell phone messages and seen the text from his bank's fraud department notifying him of a suspicious account transaction.

He'd taken over the desktop computer and typed into it, alternately speaking into the phone and yelling at Aaron.

"If you needed money, why didn't you ask me, Aaron? Why did you have to steal it?"

Aaron had been hysterical. "I didn't! I didn't touch your money. I don't need money! I just want you!"

He'd gone crazy as Dave accused him.

And now his mild-mannered husband seemed to be fighting the urge to yell once again. "They say the transfer took place at twelve-forty-five yesterday afternoon." He slammed his fist on the desk. "No wonder my card was declined at the gas station on our way back. I thought it was a computer glitch, but no. The bank froze my account!"

Aaron said nothing. They both knew he'd paid for the re-fueling with cash out of his own pocket. He thought back to the day before and how it had seemed such a fun idea sneaking away to a hotel only they knew about. They'd even let Randy think they were leaving the island. Instead, they'd crossed Kauai, traveling to the number one hotel, the Koa Kea, located in the stunning, remote Poipu area.

Now they were back to reality, or should he say, *surreality*? Nothing made a lick of sense.

Twelve-forty-five? He knew what he'd been doing then, and so did Dave.

"That proves it wasn't me!" Aaron jumped off the small rattan sofa in his office where he'd been sitting, waiting in excruciating silence as Dave ignored him. "I was with you at that exact moment, and we were in the car. We were looking at the ocean and you were fucking me! I wasn't touching my cell phone or my iPad!"

"No. No you weren't." He held up a photo. "But what was *he* doing yesterday afternoon?"

He who?" Aaron squinted at the rough image. Holy shit. It looks like me! Me and . . . oh God. It's that obnoxious artist who came to stay last year.

"Where did you get that?" He tried to snatch the photo out of Dave's hand, but Dave shook his head, whipping the image out of his reach.

"Got a whole mess of 'em left in an envelope at the front desk of the hotel. We both got one. I grabbed 'em both when we checked out since we were running late. What was that long, leisurely fuck for this morning, Aaron? A goodbye gift?"

"Goodbye? What are you talking about?"

"Guess your boyfriend can't wait. He wants you. He left the photos when neither of us responded to his emails."

"Emails?" Aaron gawked at him. This was insane. Aaron hadn't done anything. He grabbed the envelope addressed to him and ripped it open. If the photos weren't so disgusting, he'd have laughed.

"This isn't me," he said. "It's my face. But not my body. Look. The scar on my left shoulder isn't there. Whoever did this doesn't know I had that surfing accident."

Dave stared at him. "You didn't have the accident until after Skylar Blue, your paramour, left us last year."

Aaron wanted to scream and hurt somebody. "Are you sure?" He looked at the photo again. "What about the fact the room is painted blue? It was cream when he was here."

Dave sat straight in his chair. "Obviously he's been here since. Don't you want to run to him, Aaron? He's waiting." He flicked a finger at the computer monitor. "He's dying without you, quote, unquote."

Aaron felt a deep, ice-cold rage he'd never experienced before.

"Run to him? I don't even know him. He was a major pain in the ass! He complained about everything. Even the rain!"

Dave blinked. Yeah. He knew that was true.

"Google him," Aaron suddenly said.

"Google him?"

"Let's see where he is. Last time we got an email from him, you know that mass mailing he did, he was in Costa Rica painting monkeys or something."

"Lemurs." Dave templed his fingers under his chin. He didn't look up. "So what? You put that money in your account. Who knows where he is?"

"Where was the email sent from? It has to have an ISP linked to it. If he's still in Costa Rica and the email was sent from here, then it can't be him."

"I don't have time to investigate your boyfriends, Aaron. Alice told me you've fucked plenty of other guests."

"She . . . what?"

"When she called this morning and told me that she'd held

off calling me last night to mention the note she'd found here—"

"Not that again!" Aaron thought his head would explode. Randy had said he'd look after their property, but two guests had arrived from the airport the previous day and found the place deserted. They'd left a nasty note demanding a full refund, which they'd get, of course.

When he called Aaron saying he'd been beaten up, Aaron had urged him to call the cops. For some reason Randy hadn't wanted to. Randy had also begged him not to tell Dave and ruin their little mini-break but somehow Alice got the idea it had been Aaron's selfish idea to keep things quiet.

Aaron and Dave had already had a bad argument that morning about the fact Alice had called Dave and told him about the note. Now Dave revealed there was more.

"Bet this winds up on TripAdvisor too," Dave griped, holding up the nasty note their abandoned guests had left.

"Where did she get the idea I cheated on you?" Aaron was calm now. A bad moon was rising within him though. He was having crazy thoughts. He didn't know how, but he suspected—

"She said you confided in Randy and he told her. He said you've been having thoughts of suicide."

"Really? I'm planning to kill myself and run away with that lousy painter?"

Dave opened his mouth.

Aaron held up a hand to stop him. "Don't ask me how, but I know Randy Carlton isn't his real name. I know who he really is. The question is how. I just don't know how."

"How . . . what?"

"How Troy could still be alive."

Dave rolled his eyes. "Oh, come now."

"No. I'm serious. It explains everything. He's been an intrusive pest since the moment he arrived. I think I can prove it. We've got cops crawling all over the place here. We could ask them to dust for prints. And guess what? They'll find our prints, and his, all over it, because he and I have almost identical prints except for his right index finger. They call it an induced defect. Some accident with fire when we were babies that our mother could never explain."

He began warming up to his theory when there was a knock at the front door.

"Saved by the knock of sanity," Dave said, getting up from the chair. "You know what, Aaron? All of this makes sense now. Your sudden burst of seductive sex. Your new aggressiveness. Whoever brought it out of you, it wasn't me. I don't even want to look at you anymore."

He marched to the door and threw it open. Two detectives stood there.

"We've found the body of Miss Pratt. We were able to identify her through a microchip. Most of her face and extremities had been eaten away. Her body was lodged in an underwater cave. Looks like eels got to her."

"Oh, my God. Poor Genesis!" Aaron rushed over to the door. "Are you sure it's her?"

"Positive." The two detectives exchanged glances. "We'll be in touch once we've completed our investigation and an autopsy has been performed."

"Autopsy?" Aaron's throat went tight.

"Yes, why?"

"I still can't believe she's gone." He kept shaking his head. "What about her son? Does he know?"

"We've notified her family," one of the officers said. "In the meantime, I hope neither of you are planning to leave the island anytime soon."

"Why, no." Aaron was shocked at the suggestion. "We have guests arriving today. I don't know how I'll cope without her. She's . . . I mean, she was my rock."

The detectives glanced at Dave. "And you, Mr. Alvarez?'

"No. I'm not planning to leave," he said, looking miserable about that.

As soon as the officers left, Dave said, "Under the circumstances, I'm going to stay on the boat tonight."

"The boat? Why?" Aaron was devastated. He wanted a chance to explain things to Dave. To make him understand.

"I can't do this anymore, Aaron. I'm done. So done. Jesus. This shit today . . . the way you've been acting . . ."

"How have I been acting?" Aaron felt wounded—no, gutted—by these words, but any conversation was better than Dave running off to that fucking boat.

Promises.

Man, the name of it was such a bad joke.

You will be happy the fortune cookies always said.

Promises, promises.

"You and your brother are bad seeds. I don't blame you. You had the world's shittiest parents. I couldn't trust Troy and I can't trust you. I was mad to even think I could."

He lifted a hand and let it fall. He looked exhausted.

"Please, don't leave me. I love you." Aaron was desperate.

Dave's features twisted in disgust. "We'll figure out the financial stuff later but for now, I can't stand the sight of you."

"Dave, you can trust me." Aaron had no idea how he kept so calm, but he knew any hint of hysteria and Dave would go running. He hated drama.

Thanks, Troy, destroyer of dreams.

"We need to contact the Los Angeles District Attorney's office and ask them to exhume Troy's body."

"Oh, my God. You don't give up!"

"I'm telling you. I don't know how, but Randy is Troy. He's back and he wants you. And he wants me out of the way. I see the hatred in his eyes. He says I'm like a brother. Holy shit." He blinked. "I should have sensed it sooner. The dreams. Those fucking dreams."

"What dreams?" Dave sounded bored as Aaron's thoughts raced. "No, don't tell me. I actually don't care to know."

Aaron gripped Dave's arms. "Promise me, if I die . . . if something happens to me, Dave, just know I would never do something like that. I would never, ever."

Dave just looked at him. "And to think I thought you'd given up your propensity for drama."

"If I die, look to Randy. And you can bet at some point to-day he's going to call and invite you to stay and he'll poison you with lies. He's just like Troy. He's so unhappy and we all know misery loves company."

"Oh, brother." Dave went back to the office. Aaron could hear him banging around. He came back out with his wallet, cell phone, and his own laptop. "Don't call me, Aaron. Don't give me anymore bullshit about a dead man walking. When I've simmered down, we'll call our accountant."

And with that, he walked out the door.

Aaron wanted to collapse in grief, but he couldn't. Their limo was still out of commission and he had guests arriving in an hour. He didn't need to pick them up but he had two more arriving at three o'clock in the afternoon and he'd have to collect them in Dave's car.

He gazed out of the window at the beach. The police and coroner's vehicles were pulling away now. He had no chef, but that was okay. He wouldn't be making breakfast until to-morrow morning.

Aaron felt a deep, unprecedented fear of Randy. He was certain the man was Troy, and that he had instigated every-thing. He just had to prove it. He caught a movement out of the corner of his eye and jumped. Man, he saw evil in shad-ows all of a sudden. A clear, small bug was crawling up the kitchen wall.

Oh, my God.

To his horror, he realized it was a newly hatched bed bug.

He'd read that they didn't turn brown until they'd fed on a blood host. He picked up his biggest wooden spoon and cracked the insect. He killed it and examined it. It was dead. It looked like a bed bug, so he threw it down the sink. He'd read that dead female bugs had been known to shed clear babies from their sacs or something. No sense in taking any chances. He'd call the bug guys to come back and fumigate the building. He'd have to clear the place out for the day. Maybe he and Dave could take their guests out for a day-long cruise or something. *Dave . . . Man I miss him. Maybe I'll end up taking them on my own.*

He examined the wall and saw nothing else, but decided the whole place needed a good cleaning. Cleaning always made him feel better.

But I want to dust for prints.

No, Aaron. You're crazy.

He jumped when a figure loomed in the doorway.

It was Randy.

"What do you want?" he demanded, not even bothering to be polite.

Randy's lips curled into an evil sneer.

"I want what you took from me. I want my life back."

Aaron eyed the landline phone on the wall. An old-fashioned throwback, rotary phone. Perfect for emergencies, like now.

Randy gave him a harsh laugh. "You're such a loser, Aaron. Always were. Always will be. A goddamned feeb."

Aaron couldn't help it. He lunged at Randy, clearly surprising him with his punch to the face. Randy slugged him back, almost causing Aaron to black out and splitting his lip. Aaron fought back and had the absurd feeling that next Randy would tell people that Aaron had assaulted him, not his supposed ex.

Randy ducked and wove. They smashed into things, Aaron giving as good as he got.

"I'm the one who should be fucked up!" he shouted to Randy. "I'm the one that was stuck with her my whole life! You got the easy way with Dad!"

Troy went berserk then. He tried to grab Aaron, who kept ducking and weaving.

"Easy? You think I had it easy?"

"Compared with me, you did!"

Troy got him then, twisting Aaron's arm behind his back. Aaron was afraid his brother would break his arm it hurt so much. He lifted his foot and back-kicked Troy, getting him in the knee, Troy howled in pain and let him go. Aaron made a run for the door, but Troy caught his foot, tackled him and pinned him to the floor.

He straddled Aaron, putting his hands around his neck. The rage Aaron saw in his brother's face was palpable.

"She abused me when we were babies," Troy said. "That's why Dad took me away."

Aaron knew this, but she'd abused him, too.

"She raped me," he told his brother, "and still I got stuck with her."

The two brothers stared at each other.

"We could have been friends. Instead you tried to steal my husband!" Troy's hands tightened around Aaron's neck.

Aaron tried to fight but his brother had a grip like steel.

"No. I won't finish it this way." Troy eased his hold but didn't let go. "I tried to give you a taste of the good life, Aaron."

"No, Troy. You tried to set me up as the fall guy. You left me to deal with all the shit you started."

Troy laughed. "When did you know it was me?"

Aaron had a feeling it bugged Troy that Aaron knew.

"It was gradual, but it's a quirk you have. Something I knew."

"What quirk?" Troy looked frantic now. He started

tightening his hold again, but they could hear footsteps outside. "I'll be back. You'll see. When you least expect it, you'll meet with a common household accident." He moved his hands from Aaron's throat then got to his feet, dragging the back of his hand across his mouth.

"You got me, Aaron," he whispered when blood streaked across his skin from his lips. "I'm so going to enjoy watching you die."

He left as quickly as he came.

Aaron lay there, trying to breathe, wondering who would believe him, how he could stop Troy before he met with his 'little accident.'

The footsteps turned out to be pesky Alice.

"Oh, my!" she said when she saw Aaron's face. "Did your husband do that to you?"

"Randy did it," he said. He got to his feet. He made mental lists and began to clean. If he was going to die, then he needed to organize some things. But first, there were guests to pamper and care for.

"Your kitchen's a mess," she said.

Thank you, helpful Hannah.

"Yes, I know. Anything I can do for you?"

"Well, I was wondering. Now that your marriage is over, will you be listing the property or . . ." She glanced around uncertainly.

Aaron fought to keep his composure. Boy, she was something else.

"My marriage isn't over." He gave her a sweet smile. "And we're not selling. I've put every ounce of my life's blood in this—"

"Your husband told me it was over."

Aaron's heart sank. When had Dave seen her? He said he wanted to go sit on the stupid boat.

"I just want to say, when the time comes, please . . . consider me. I love this property." Under his withering gaze, she began to stammer. "I . . . I . . . know its worth and everything you've done. I could—"

"Fuck off, Alice!"

She sighed. "I'll just um . . . I'll leave my card here. Just in case." She left it on the kitchen bench top and walked quickly away from the house.

Aaron waited a moment then sprang into action. Running on sheer adrenaline, he spent some time lifting prints off the kitchen door where he had seen Troy touching the frame. He lifted them off with adhesive tape and stuck each piece onto a sheet of tabletop glass he kept on hand for the service tables outside. He'd lifted enough pieces to cover a twelve-inch piece of glass and gently put it in the safe. He also made copies of his own prints and put them on a separate piece of glass, leaving that in the safe. Next, he wrote a note to Dave telling him everything and how he'd put it together. He couldn't do much else right now. Not with guests coming. He put the note in the safe and locked the door again.

He cleaned the kitchen and left the spaces he'd lifted prints from the doorframe for evidence. He had no doubt his brother would kill him, but he had no idea how. He'd have to keep his wits about him and be vigilant. He cut some red Lokelani roses in the garden for his female guest. He loved this island strain of roses. They were fragrant and lacy in appearance. They looked like peonies before they opened. They had another quality too. They were impervious to island insects and disease.

Aaron took a moment to survey his garden. Everything they'd worked for, touched—every ounce of love . . . it was all here. Tangible. David couldn't possibly look at this and believe Aaron was anything other than devoted.

He forced himself to press on. Mrs. Halliday's welcome flip-flops had rose embellishments to match her passion for roses. Her husband's had a fishing tackle motif. They were coming on their second honeymoon and like most of Aaron and Dave's other guests, had been kind enough to answer the questionnaire on what their favorite flowers, candy, and food were.

Aaron checked the bathroom for the skin and hair care products he provided. He looked at his face in the mirror. He had a fat lip and an expression of deceptive calm in his eyes. He couldn't help thinking of the Michael Jackson song, 'Man in the Mirror.'

He couldn't help thinking the mirror was supposed to reflect what the world saw. Then, if that were true, then he was defeated.

And he felt anything but defeated.

Aaron forced his gaze away and left the bathroom. The sweet smell of the island roses filled his spirits. And then the words came to his mind.

No roses for a sailor's grave.

He took a deep breath. *Water.* He got a glimpse in his mind of water. *My God, it's just like the dream. A scarf. My falling overboard. No. Pushed. He's going to push me off the boat. He's going to drown me. All my life I've had a fear of drowning.*

Aaron forced himself to complete his tasks. He'd picked a few extra Lokelanis but he wouldn't put them in the living room. He'd take those to his and Dave's room later. He tried not to think that Dave might really have left him. He shook his head, as though to loosen his dark thoughts.

He liked to make his guests feel special, so they got their own flowers. He'd picked some heliconia and bird of paradise blooms for the common areas. They looked spectacular in his large, red crystal vases.

He wanted bright. He wanted red. The color of love. The color of blood.

No roses for a sailor's grave . . .

From outside, he could hear a car-horn honking. He straightened his shoulders, tried to neaten his hair with slightly shaky fingers and started to go outside to greet his guests. He stopped himself in his tracks. There were no *leis* in the fridge. That distressed him. He'd never welcomed a single guest without a flower greeting.

Wait. There were two *leis* in the house. The ones the Koa Kea had given him and Dave. It tore his heart to do it, but they were exquisite *leis* and Dave would surely understand their guests deserved a proper taste of Pineapple Hill *aloha*.

He opened his travel bag that stood in his office right where he'd left it when they'd first come home and took out the two Ziploc bags. Another honk. His fingers shook as he unwrapped the *leis* from the pieces of wet newspaper he'd wrapped them in before putting them in plastic. It was an old island trick Genesis had taught him.

Genesis. He grieved for her, shocked to the core at the idea of never seeing his beloved mentor and friend again. The *leis* were perfect. He slung them over his arm and ran outside.

His guests were unloading their bags from the trunk of their rental SUV.

"*Aloha!*" he shouted.

"*Aloha!*" They returned his greeting.

Aaron put the flower garlands around their necks.

"My goodness, this is beautiful. What is this green flower?" Mrs. Halliday held it to her nose and inhaled.

"We call it a pearl ginger orchid. It's a hybrid created right here on this island." He turned to Mr. Halliday. "Here, please let me help you."

He lifted two of the suitcases. Man, they were heavy. What did people bring to the islands for a week, anyway?

"Are we the only ones here?" Mrs. Halliday asked, as he led the way to their room, The *Pikake* Suite. It had its own bathroom and a balcony overlooking the old pineapple plantation.

"Yes, you are. We're expecting another couple this

afternoon," he said.

"Oh, these roses are lovely." Mrs. Halliday removed her *lei* and to his horror, he saw that she'd dropped it into the waste basket. Her husband, a little more gracious than she, placed his over one of the bedposts.

Aaron could tell she was already going to be a pain in the ass. She cast a critical eye over everything.

"We require coffee all throughout the day," she said. "I thought we'd made that clear."

"Yes. There's an insulated four cup carafe in the hallway with. As soon as you've finished it, I'd be happy to make more."

She gave him an unsatisfied look and brushed past him.

He followed her to the hallway where she found the *koa* wood sideboard with coffee, creamer, sugar, and his usual two styles of water. He'd also left a covered plate of home-made coconut ginger cookies and homemade cheese wafers. She glanced at the fruit bowl filled with oranges, bananas, grapes, and tiny Molokai apples.

"I guess this will do," she said, but he noticed she picked up two cookies and gobbled them the moment his back had turned.

"Is there anything else I can get you, Mrs. Halliday?"

"What time is lunch?"

"I'm sorry, we don't serve lunch. We have this spread, and at five, we will serve cocktails and canapés."

"And that's all?"

"There's breakfast tomorrow," he said. Why was she being so grumpy?

She stalked off again and he retreated to the kitchen. Man, this is going to hell fast. I hate this. He brushed the thought aside.

Mrs. Halliday came into the kitchen. "Where's the pool?"

"There is no pool. We have natural mineral baths and a

Jacuzzi."

"I thought there was a pool."

"I'm sorry, no. We're right on the beach."

"I hate the ocean."

Okay then. He waited until she'd left before scanning the list of things he needed. He added coffee and *leis* and pocketed the page.

He would pick up what he needed from the Wainiha General Store. Maybe he'd even pick up a couple of sandwiches, if the Hallidays wanted them. He returned to their room, but they had fallen asleep, fully clothed, on their bed.

Carefully locking up, he drove to the store, picked up what he needed, trying to feel disgruntled at the cheesy *lei* offerings they had in the walk-in fridge. The deep floral smell lifted his sagging psyche and he lingered inside for a moment before taking the remains of their hand-strung garlands to the counter. He paid with his own money, not the company card. Lord knew if that even worked anymore.

He hated to think about none of this being his anymore. He couldn't lose his life. He paid for his purchases, knowing he was paying a little extra for the convenience of the place. He didn't care. One more set of guests to arrive.

Maybe all this would blow over.

And maybe, just maybe, pigs would fly as hell froze over.

He drove home, his senses heightened, but everything was okay. He arrived home and his guests still slumbered. He put everything away then took the roses he'd picked for next door to his bedroom and walked inside, letting out a sigh when he saw that it had been trashed.

Aaron checked his watch. Enough was enough. He left the roses and went back outside. He drove to the police station, determined to report Randy's abusive intrusion and his constant harassment. There was a police station at Hanalei Bay. They wouldn't believe him, probably. He'd sound like a dope.

He made a left turn and a big truck came out of nowhere. He squinted. He could see the driver was wearing a balaclava. A balaclava in Kaui!

Aaron tried to step on the gas as he rounded the curve of the five-sixty highway. The truck got closer and closer, honking hard. The driver honked nonstop now as he sped up and hit Aaron.

Where were other cars? Where were the cops?

Too late, he skidded at a hairpin turn, plunged right into a guard rail and with a terrified scream, plunged over the cliff, the rocks and water below greeting him as he crashed into the foamy waves.

CHAPTER SEVEN

This poor little island hadn't seen this much action in like . . . never. First, poor Genesis, then that nice little B and B owner, Aaron, had plunged off a bridge. Suicide. He'd been cheating on his boyfriend, and when the boyfriend left and threatened to take everything . . . well what was a poor B and B owner to do, but to kill himself? Tragedy all the way . . . Shakespeare would have really dug this place.

Too bad about the truck driver though. He was in the wrong place at the wrong time, colliding with a reckless and distraught young man bent on ending his pain. Driver had a wife and kiddies, too. He'd shown Troy the pictures at the gas station. Really cute. The youngest, little Tammy, was turning five next week and poor Roger, he said he was sure he'd make it home in time for cake and ice cream. Oh well. At least Roger had been dead before he hit the water.

Troy had cut it close though, jumping out at the last minute onto the road. He could have been killed as well, but it was worth all the risk because in the distance, Troy could see David sitting on the deck of *The Promise*.

So, all was not tragedy on this sweet little island. Troy's eyes filled with tears. Finally, David was his again. And it was perfect, just perfect. Everything David and he would ever need was on that boat. They could sail anywhere they wanted. They had the money, and they had each other. That's all that mattered.

It was just too bad Troy was so battered and bruised right now. The rough sex he'd fantasized about with David might have to be a little tamer until he healed.

Troy began to hurry now. He glanced up at the sky and saw the sun sink below the horizon. He wanted to be off. Maybe they could leave tonight. Troy just needed to convince David he didn't need that loser, Aaron, and get them out of here before he found out his beloved was at the bottom of the sea.

David looked up as Troy approached. Troy knew he'd be hurting. That's okay. He'd indulge him for a bit, get him over whatever, but he wouldn't tolerate his moaning for more than a day or two. He deserved some attention from David after all the trouble he'd gone to just for him. A little payback wasn't too much to ask, was it?

Troy stepped onto the deck and gave David a compassionate smile. "Look at us," Troy said, raising his arms, "two peas in a pod, it looks like."

"How do you figure that?" David asked, his deep voice calm and solemn. He was looking out at the water.

David's jean clad legs were stretched out, crossed at the ankles on the guard rail. He wore a light blue, cotton shirt . . . almost the same colour as his eyes. It was blowing open around his taut, muscular chest, his dark hair brushed his cheek. The first thing that had struck Troy about David when he first saw the man, aside from his perfect body and substantial cock was the coal black hair and bronzed skin set against his incredible blue eyes. No wonder he'd gone to all this trouble, looking like a wounded soldier for the guy.

Troy moved a little closer then leaned against the cabin. "Look at us. I've been abused by my ex and so have you. Poor David. I'm so sorry. I should have said something before."

Those eyes turned to him. Troy caught his breath. They sparkled. "When did you know that Aaron was sleeping around?" David asked.

"Aaron confessed something like that to me. I was so

distraught. I mean how could he do that to someone like you?"

"It's not the first time," David said, meeting Troy's gaze.

"Oh?" Troy looked around.

"It seems I haven't had much luck with men."

"Well, luck can change."

"Um, let's hope," David said softly.

"I spoke to Alice about Aaron, and I shouldn't have. I didn't realize she was such a gossip. I needed someone to talk to, just like you do now, David. I want you to know I'm here for you in every way."

"In every way?" He looked at him again.

Troy's heartbeat sped up a little. "Well . . . in any way you need, of course. As a friend or . . ."

"A friend," David repeated. He tilted his head. "What if what I need tonight is more than friendship, Randy? What if I need to fuck . . . all night long . . . not to think about the man I've come to love with everything I have in my soul? Would you be there for me like that as well?" David lowered his feet to the deck and stood.

Troy was breathless. This was going to be far easier than he thought. "A man like you," Troy began, "has needs, needs that maybe Aaron couldn't fulfil." Troy moved a little closer. *Not too fast. You'll scare him off. Easy Troy boy . . . he's yours . . . like a fine stallion . . . can't be spooked.*

David shook his head with a faint smile. "I need a drink. Why don't we have one together inside?"

Troy nodded. He put a hand on David's shoulder. "It will be all right, my friend. I'll help you through this."

"Oh . . ." David glanced back at him. "I know it will all right. I plan to take care of everything tonight."

"Now, I didn't much like the sound of that. Don't do anything rash, David."

"Oh, it's not rash at all," he replied. "It's been a long time coming."

"It won't do to get in trouble for Aaron."

"I wouldn't think of that," David answered, walking over to the bar.

Troy glanced around the luxury boat as Troy took a seat. He was anxious to check out his hiding place, but he knew the money would still be there. "I'll have a . . ."

"Gin and tonic with a touch a lemon." David cut him off, turning around with the drink in his hand.

"That's incredible," Troy remarked, eyes widening. "How did you know that was my drink?"

David shrugged. He didn't pour himself a drink. Instead he stood there a few feet away, looking at him. "Didn't you drink that back at the house?"

"Maybe. Aren't you drinking?" Troy took a sip of his.

"No, changed my mind." He walked over and sat down beside Troy. "I need to keep a clear head tonight."

Troy touched his hand. "You're incredible, you know that. Maybe you didn't really love this guy. Maybe it's a relief to be rid of him. Most men in your position would be drinking like nuts."

"Um, perhaps. Is that what you did?" David asked.

Troy took another sip of the drink. "Is that what I did, when?"

"Is that what you did . . . drink like crazy when it was over . . . with Russ I mean?"

"No. Russ meant very little to me. I was never in love with Russ."

"Not like your husband."

"Oh, yes . . . that . . . well . . . that's over too." Troy laughed. Had he spoken about that to David? No, he didn't think so.

"How convenient for you that everything is all wrapped up."

Troy narrowed his eyes. He put down the drink. "People get over stuff, just like you'll get over Aaron eventually. And

I have just the solution."

David leaned back against the sofa. Troy moved a little closer, touched his cheek.

"Oh?" David murmured. "And what is that solution, Randy?"

"I want to kiss you. Do you mind?"

David reached out and yanked Troy roughly up to his chest. *Oh yeah, that's my boy!*

"Whoa!" Troy giggled. "That sudden motion made my head spin." In fact, the entire room was spinning.

"Aren't you going to finish your drink?" David said, his mouth so close to Troy's, Troy could already taste it. "I made it just for you."

Troy strained closer but David's lips didn't quite touch his.

"I've had enough. Why don't you take off those jeans?" Troy suggested. He pushed in for a kiss again, but suddenly David was standing in front of him.

"Good idea," David said. "Let's go to the bedroom."

Troy stumbled up and staggered after David. David turned on the lamp. There was something sitting on the bed, a box. Troy went closer, then his eyes widened. He looked at David, who was standing a few feet away. "Where did you . . . what is that?"

David smiled. "It's our future, isn't it?"

"I don't understand. What's in it?" Troy feigned ignorance.

"Open it and find out."

Troy dropped down on the bed and opened the box. "Money," he smiled. He glanced up again. "Is it yours?"

"No." David shook his head. "It's yours . . . or . . . the mob's."

"Mob?" Troy swallowed hard. "Really? Where did you find this?"

"In the place you've always hidden things . . . like the pictures you took of me when you insisted on that little sex romp with call boys in our hotel room that time. Cuba, wasn't it?"

"I . . . I don't . . . understand." Troy shook his head. He couldn't know. He couldn't.

"Then let me enlighten you," David replied, his voice still calm. "You see, before Aaron, I was married to another man."

"I heard a rumor."

"Did you now?" David gave Troy a smile. In the lamplight, it looked sinister.

"You were married to Aaron's twin. I heard he died."

"Um, me too." David sighed. "So sad."

Troy put the money box on the night table. "Come and sit down, tell me all about it." Troy patted the bed.

"Oh, it's a . . ." David sucked in some breath. "You wouldn't believe this story if I told you."

"I would. Go on."

"Well . . . I was seduced and manipulated by Troy. He pretended to love me, but he constantly cheated on me with other men. And he got involved with some mobsters . . . stole some money . . . he had everything then he got scared. He set up his twin to take the fall for his crimes."

"David, I'm sure he really loved you. I'm sure he regretted everything and that if he could do it again . . ." Troy looked up at David, who'd come to the side of the bed. "He would." The motion of the water rocking the boat was making him feel ill. Why was David's face blurry now?

David reached down and stroked his hair roughly then he took his chin in his hand and forced Troy to look up at him. "Well . . . sometimes there is no going back, my love. Sometimes . . . things can't be forgiven. You took a gamble and you lost." David's face turned dark.

"What? What are you saying . . . David?"

David's hand reached out for him. Troy was pulled off the bed and onto the floor. David seemed to be holding him up. "Did you really think one could be married to a man and not fucking recognize him eventually? You used me before. You used your brother. And you know what I've figured out after all this time? I'm the only one who can truly punish you, Troy, because in spite of everything, I'm the only one you've ever cared about."

Troy gasped. "No! I'm not . . . why did you call me that?" He heard himself screaming it over and over. "Troy is dead, David . . . dead!"

David was dragging him through the cabin and up the stairs.

"We can have it . . . all . . . the money. Everything. David, what are you doing? Where are you taking me? No! No!" Troy tried to fight but something had weakened him. "The drink," he gasped, "you put . . . something . . . in my . . . drink!"

David pulled Troy over to the guard rail. Somehow now the boat was floating . . . No longer anchored, they were drifting on the water. Or maybe he was just imagining it was. When had David taken them out? Had he blacked out? Everything was a blur. He felt a sharp pull on his hair then David pushed him to his knees in front of him.

Troy looked up at him. "I . . . love you." He gulped, his chest heaving.

"Strange thing is, Troy, I know that." He nodded. David's face seemed to crumble for a moment, some emotion gripped him. His voice shook a little when he spoke. "There was a time when I really loved you too, Troy. I would have done anything for you, even forgiven all your sexual indiscretions if you had promised to stop it. But . . . it was Aaron all along I should have been with and by some twist of fate, some random choice at birth, I ended up with the monster."

"Please, David," Troy sobbed. He clutched at David's legs. "Please, it's different now . . . I have learned . . . so much, I've grown . . . I've . . ."

"You've taken everything from me." David's voice got

louder now, laced with anger. "Everything!" David's face faded in and out. "And now it's time to put a dead man back in his grave!"

Troy was brought to his feet and turned around in David's arms. David held him with Troy's back to his chest. For a moment, it was comforting. Troy closed his eyes, remembering the warmth of David's arms. A single tear ran down his cheek. The boat rocked and the night sky seemed to mock him with the glittery sky above, the perfect moon. He felt David's rough jaw rub against cheek and his breath whisper against his ear. A deep sense of need and longing gripped him.

"I do love you," he told David. And that was why his final act had to save David from all Troy had done. "I can't let you rot in prison for this, David." Troy sighed. The thought of that, the thought that his David would spend the rest of his life behind bars was too much for him to accept.

"That doesn't matter," David told him. "It's time I took care of things."

Troy wondered if he had the strength. One hard push was all it would take. It would give him time to do what he had to do. Perhaps it was going to end as it should. Finally, he and Aaron would wind up in the sea together, the mirrored sides united, once and for all.

"I can't." Troy tasted tears in his mouth. "I can't . . . I need to do one . . . thing . . . for all the pain I caused you . . . to show you . . . I love you so much, David."

Troy felt David's chest heave. He was crying. Troy smiled. Perhaps just one of those tears was because of him . . . shed for the fleeting moments they'd had together before he'd fucked everything up. "You're my only regret," he whispered. "Oh David, I can't let you suffer any more for me."

One big push back, a push David didn't expect. Troy felt David's hold on him release. He took one long look at David, who was rising from where he was sprawled on deck. "It was always you," he yelled over the sounds of the wind and the waves then he mounted the guardrail, glancing down at the water. It wasn't his reflection that looked back at him anymore, it was Aaron's. They were no longer a mirror image.

He heard someone shout his name. "Troy!" And then he scrambled over the guard rail and dropped.

Aaron watched in horror as Troy threw himself overboard. Beside him on the police launch were the two detectives who'd miraculously come to his rescue as he'd fought to release himself from his car.

"Your husband called us," they'd said. "He was worried Randy Carlton would try and kill you."

Dave rushed over to edge of the *Promises*, his gaze only on Aaron, not the floundering Troy, thrashing about in the water.

The two Coast Guard officers on the launch jumped into the water to go after Troy. Absurdly, Troy didn't want their help. He kept kicking and hitting at them to keep them at bay.

Aaron had never seen a man so determined to die. When Troy's body went limp, Aaron returned Dave's stare. *Lord, I love this man.*

"I love you!" David shouted.

"I love you, too!" It was what had kept him alive when he'd hit the water. In spite of his terror, Aaron had been surprised that an article he'd read on what to do if your car becomes submerged in water came back to him. He'd kept his wits about him. He kept his seatbelt on and before the car's fuses shorted, he pressed the window lever so the window opened. It only went halfway but it was plenty.

He'd fought his total panic and the images of his life flashing before his eyes as he waited for the water to fill the vehicle. It came faster than he expected but when it reached chest level, he released the seatbelt and he popped up, like a cork, making him able to evacuate through the window. It hadn't been pain-free. He'd bashed his head on the door frame and had further damaged his torn lip.

But I'm alive. We're free.

It tore at Aaron to see his husband's face twisted with such grief.

"Get over here!" Dave yelled, then before Aaron could respond, plunged into the water. Aaron and a Coast Guard officer leaned down to help him climb up the ladder on the side of the craft.

Aaron clung to him as Dave clambered on board. For a long time, they lay sprawled on the deck.

"I'm sorry. I'm sorry," Dave kept saying. "I had to let Randy think I believed all those lies about you. I had to get him out here to the boat."

The cops kept asking questions. Dave and Aaron got to his feet as Troy's body was hauled on board.

"He's dead," one of the detectives said. "He can't hurt you anymore."

"Good," Dave barked back. "He should have stayed dead the first time." He pointed to the *Promises*. "In the master bedroom you'll find a box with all the pictures he's kept of the time we were married. He must have come on board earlier and put it in the cabinet under the bathroom sink. I guess he was already making himself at home. He didn't think I'd see it, but I did. I'd never seen the box before. I opened it and found it was filled with money. I guessed it was money from a heist back in LA and he admitted it was."

"*He* had the money?" Aaron was in shock. "All this time?"

Dave shrugged. "I counted the bills. It was the exact amount that was missing."

Aaron couldn't believe it. *All this time . . .*

"I think he hid the money under the cabinet," Dave said. "I could be wrong, but I found the board was loose. I think he came looking for it."

He hugged Aaron again.

"Mr. Alvarez," one of the detectives said, "we're going to have to process the boat. We'll let you have access to it in a few days."

Dave waved off the man's words. "Keep the damned thing as long as you like. It's got nothing but bad memories for us."

Aaron realized Dave was right. It had been Troy's boat, and it had helped them escape LA. But for Troy it was a tool of manipulation. Aaron tried hard to feel relaxed now it was all over.

The detectives took them back to shore on the launch and once on dry land, drove them back to Pineapple Hill. He and Dave had stayed silent the whole trip, but the detectives had talked nonstop.

Aaron listened with mounting astonishment as he heard that his insane twin had been caught via secret hotel room monitors murdering an LAPD detective before heading to Hawaii. The hotel owner had watched the whole thing on taped delay. According to the Kauai detectives, the hotel owner had installed the cameras to spy on unsuspecting female guests. One of them had found a camera and complained. To avoid jail time, he'd offered up the cop's murder footage in exchange for immunity.

Dave seemed distraught when the police told them how Randy/Troy had used the fallen cop's money to buy his house in Kauai.

Aaron was worried about his husband's profound silence as they rolled into the driveway of the bed and breakfast.

No cars. The limo's still in for service and Dave's car is ruined. Oh, my God. We had guests arriving at three!

Aaron peered at the two couples clustered outside as they got out of the police vehicle. Mrs. Halliday could see that Aaron and Dave were in bad shape but began whining that they'd run out of coffee hours ago.

"Please, they've had a harrowing day," one of the cops told her. She stopped talking but Aaron knew her type. She probably only stopped complaining when she fell asleep.

He and Dave clung to one another. "Mr. and Mrs. Peachtree?" Aaron asked the second couple, who nodded. "I'm sorry I didn't pick you up, but I had a little accident."

"We heard it on the news. Are you all right?" the woman asked.

Aaron glanced at Dave. "I will be, thank you."

Dave tightened his hold on Aaron. "If you'll excuse us for a few moments, we'd like to shower and change then we'll make you the best island cocktails you've ever tasted."

"Wonderful!" Mrs. Peachtree exclaimed.

"If you say so," Mrs. Halliday muttered.

Back in their room, Dave stared with dismay at the wreckage created no doubt by Troy. "I saw this before I left," he told Aaron. "As soon as I saw this, I knew, just *knew* that Randy was really Troy. You know, when we were married and we had fights, this was the type of crap he pulled. He'd go berserk destroying things. He'd always be apologetic later, but . . ." He stopped speaking and frowned.

"What is it?" Aaron asked.

"Oh . . . it just occurred to me that he was the one who trashed the cottage that day."

"Yeah. I think he did, too." Aaron peeled off his clothes and walked into the bathroom. A part of him was grateful and relieved that their ordeal was over. Another part was still jumpy and suspicious. That would ease with time. He glanced at his reflection in the mirror. No more fear. That was gone. In its place, a tired, sad, hungry, but happy man.

They say the way to all change starts with the man in the mirror. I am going to start with me. I am fully committed to making my husband happy, putting the past behind us. The deadly weed in our garden is gone. I can look back and grieve, or look forward and laugh . . .

Dave came up behind him, wrapping his arms around him. They traded glances in the mirror.

"We have to be quick. That Mrs. Halliday's a piece of work, isn't she?"

Aaron laughed. "She sure is."

They jumped into the shower and took turns washing one another. Their smiles grew stronger. So did their erections.

"I hate to take a rain check on this but . . ." He kept touching and stroking Aaron's cock.

Aaron pulled away. "How am I supposed to pull my pants up over this?" he griped, giving Dave a wink.

Back in the bed and breakfast, Dave, Pineapple Hill's official cocktail king, entertained their guests with his moves behind the bar. Aaron kept thinking about his man's moves in the bedroom. *Don't think about that now. Concentrate.*

He found the last of some frozen *spanakopita*, cheese and spinach triangles, and threw them in the oven. His cell phone rang. It was Alice. Aaron didn't think he was ready for his least favorite gossip, but he took the call.

"Aaron! I've just heard everything. My God. What a nightmare! The police think he may have killed Genesis! They say he killed the driver of the truck that ran you off the road."

He almost hung up on her when she said, "You're going to be busier than ever! You're going to have hordes coming here, and you'll need help. It's all over the news about Randy, or should I call him Troy? Anyway, Franklin is still looking for a cook's job and I think he's perfect for you. He's a former Marine and he could be a bit of extra security—"

"Yes," Aaron said. "I'm sorry, we have guests and I need to tend to them. Please tell him to come as quickly as possible."

"Well, he's here," Alice said. "He's staying with me." She paused. "Have you given any thought to what you want to do with your brother's house?"

"My brother's—" He bit off an angry retort. "I'm sure it must go to the family of the man he murdered."

Alice fell silent, but only briefly. "Why, yes. Of course. I hadn't considered that."

"I have to go," Aaron said. He ended their call on her cheery goodbye and shook his head over Alice's one-track mind. He was astonished fifteen minutes later when she rolled up in the driveway with Franklin, who didn't look like a gourmet chef. He looked like a Marine with a heavy body-building obsession.

Franklin looked relieved to be out of Alice's clutches as she sashayed into the living room to join the party.

"Please, leave your kit over here and I'll show you your cottage later. Would you like a drink?" Aaron asked.

"Sure thing," Franklin said.

Aaron pulled out the pastries, fretting that they didn't have enough food. He was an improvisational kind of cook and after taking Franklin to the others, passed around a tray of food. He returned to the kitchen and quickly began making mushroom caps and cheese toast points. They had a ton of crudités in the fridge, so he whipped up a batch of green goddess dressing, and almost wept.

Genesis had taught him her secret recipe. He took a deep breath and returned to the living room with his latest offerings. Dave had wisely put Keola Beamer on the sound system. Even Mrs. Halliday was smiling. It was hard to be a bitch with Keola singing in your ear.

"This dressing is divine," she trilled. "You must share the recipe with me."

"I will," he said.

Back in the kitchen, Dave walked up behind him, giving

him a jolt.

"Sorry," Aaron said.

Dave took him in his arms. "Don't be." He kissed the top of Aaron's head. "Are you okay? You look kinda beat up. Did you see a doctor after the crash?"

"The paramedics came. Said I'd have a nasty headache for a couple of days. And actually, I do have a bad headache."

Dave looked pained. "No more cooking. It's enough. You've dazzled everyone with your prowess. I'm going to make you a really stiff, tasty Mai Tai, take you to bed, and take advantage of you."

"Is that so?" Aaron laughed. "But I'm a willing seductee. If there's such a word."

Dave laughed too, and took his hand.

Back in the living room, everyone looked comfy. Mrs. Halliday was sharing her enthusiasm for The Blue Book and how she'd bought the guide for each and every island.

Dave and Aaron exchanged glances as she confided her desire to try out Kipu Falls.

"Have you been there?" she asked Franklin, who shook his head. The conversation went on. Aaron couldn't really contribute much. He'd hit a wall of exhaustion and Dave's amazing cocktail helped soothe the blunt edges of his headache. He sipped until Dave took his hand and bidding the others a goodnight, let him lead him away.

Back in their room, Aaron so badly wanted his husband, but the second they hit the sheets, he fell asleep.

Aaron awoke around four, aware of Dave moving around the room.

"What are you doing?" he asked, feeling groggy." It was hard to lift his head off the pillow.

"We've got a house full of party people," Dave said. "They

finally just went to bed."

Aaron rose on one elbow with difficulty and watched Dave getting dressed.

"I'm going to clean up the house, stack the dishwasher, and turn off all the lights," Dave said. "When you get up, the kitchen will be all yours."

"Hell, no." Aaron swung his legs over the bed. "I'm helping you."

"No, you're not. I felt that lump on top of your head. You've got a dinosaur egg going on there. You still have that headache?"

Aaron reluctantly nodded.

Dave touched his cheek. "I'll tell you what. I'll wake you at six forty-five. You can get Franklin out of his room. He was the last to turn in judging by the noise out there. Thank God we don't have any neighbors. We're gonna have to talk to him about what we expect."

"Okay," Aaron said, allowing himself to sink into sleep again.

At six thirty, which felt like a few seconds after their conversation, Dave gently shook him awake. "Come for a swim," he urged. "You can make breakfast while I handle the business stuff and as soon as everyone's fed, you and I will sneak back here for a hot and sexy rendezvous."

"Dave," Aaron said, leaning up to wind his arms around his man's neck. "You always have such great ideas."

They kissed for a moment, threw on their shorts, then walked down to the beach. Aaron felt the thrill of being alive on such a crystal clear, golden morning in their little pocket of paradise. No more pesky neighbor. He drew in a deep breath, releasing it with a thousand thanks to the universe. Dave held his hand as they ran into the sea together. The water was icy cold and wonderful.

The two men frolicked, and Aaron reluctantly left his

husband to his solitary run along the sand.

"Wake me up earlier tomorrow," Aaron said before Dave took off. "I want to run with you."

Dave gave him a slow smile. "You sure?"

Aaron held his gaze. "Very sure." He ran back to the house, showered, threw on fresh shorts and a T-shirt, and went to rouse Franklin who was really hung over.

"I've cooked in worse shape," he assured Aaron.

Back in the kitchen, Aaron prepared the coffee, inhaling the scent of the pure Kona grounds. He swallowed a couple of aspirin to help with the headache then began squeezing a ton of fruit for juice. Next, he prepared their last loaf of Portuguese bread, dredging the slices in an egg and Cointreau mixture and let it soak for a few minutes in a deep dish.

Franklin started to fry bacon and Portuguese sausages in a large skillet. Suddenly he said, "I think I'm going to be sick," and ran out of the kitchen door.

Aaron rolled his eyes as Franklin barfed into the bushes in the driveway. Then he heard Mrs. Halliday's shrill "Yoohoo!" and cringed.

"Where's my coffee?" she called out from the hallway. Aaron poked his head through the door and said, "It's coming up, Mrs. Halliday. Just making it now."

He wondered how far along the beach Dave was. He felt like running away and joining him right now.

"Do I smell something burning?" Mrs. Halliday trilled.

Aaron dashed to the stove and rescued the meat just in time, putting the sizzling pieces onto paper towels to soak up the grease. He dipped the French toast pieces into the batter and slid them onto another skillet.

On a roll now, he whipped a dozen eggs with a little water and some fresh tarragon and rosemary from the garden and began scrambling them in his cast iron pan.

Mrs. Halliday kept whining, so he poured the coffee from

the French press into a carafe and handed it to her. He began preparing a second pot, feeling proud of himself for keeping his act together.

"Is that what you're making?" she asked. "I expected a gourmet breakfast."

He gritted his teeth as she disappeared. An embarrassed-looking Franklin returned, and Aaron's tension eased somewhat. Breakfast was always served at seven thirty and ended at nine thirty. As the two couples tucked into their meals, Aaron joined them at the table, enjoying their appreciative comments. He'd made enough food to feed an army. Mrs. Halliday must have thought she was one, because she shoveled food into her mouth as one might feed coal to a furnace. He sipped his coffee, while eating a sliced papaya drizzled with fresh lime juice.

"Just so lovely. Perfect," Mrs. Peachtree said. She was lovely and perfect, too.

"Can you recommend a romantic restaurant for dinner?" she asked Aaron.

He smiled at her. "Without a doubt, it's the Beach House."

"Oh." Her face fell. "We tried getting a reservation there. They are booked solid."

"Leave it with me," he said.

"Really?" Her eyes shone.

"Yes, really. What time?"

"We were hoping for seven."

"Consider it done." He'd get this lovely and gracious couple into that restaurant if he had to do favors for the Maitre D' for the rest of his life. He owed the Peachtrees for not being able to collect them at the airport.

"By the way," Mrs. Halliday announced, talking right over Mrs. Peachtree's heartfelt thanks. "I hope you'll be doing a better job of keeping the coffee hot and fresh today."

"Yes," he said. "I'll try not to have any near-fatal collisions.

Just for you."

Mr. Halliday looked mortified and tried to cover the awkward moment by asking Aaron if he had tried Tidepools restaurant.

"David adores that place," Aaron responded, making a mental note to book a table there as a surprise for David on Sunday night, their favorite night to dine out.

"I read on Yelp that the *koi* fish sometimes jump out of their ponds and land at your feet," Mr Halliday said. "Do they really do that?"

Aaron shrugged. "Frequently. It's happened to me a time or two, but they're easy to catch and you throw them right back in."

"Ugh," Mrs. Halliday announced dramatically.

The others ignored her and began to relax, chattering and swapping travel tips. Dave joined them. Aaron thrilled at the sight of his husband as David handed Aaron the list of incoming guests. Three more today.

That would mean a shopping trip to replenish their low food stocks, but not yet. Not until he got his hands on Dave.

Mrs. Halliday was complaining to her husband about his lack of driving skills, the fact that she didn't like tropical fruit, and why, oh why, did she keep having to ask for more coffee?

Aaron could tell the Peachtrees hated her. Suddenly, she turned to Aaron. "You never did tell me what you think of the Kipu Falls," she said in an accusatory tone. "What do you think? Do you recommend them?"

Normally, he said no. But he suspected she was the type who would take offense at any suggestion that she should avoid a place. She was probably the type who would see the two dirt roads leading to the falls and take the one that was marked with trespassing signs. She'd be safe, but the furious homeowners whose properties bisected the trail would not.

I wish I could be a fly on the wall when she bitches and

moans at them.

"Mrs. Halliday, I think it's a splendid walk," he said, watching the expression of astonishment on his husband's face.

He got up from the table and found Franklin in the kitchen with his head in the sink. "Take the day off, after you've cleared the table," Aaron said, giving his shoulder a comforting pat. "I'll do the dishes later."

Aaron ran next door, aware of Dave's footsteps behind him.

"There's a little Troy in you, sweetheart," Dave said, laughing in the sanctity of their bedroom. "Fancy telling her that treacherous trail is a splendid walk!"

Aaron laughed. "I bet she never even gets out of the car. She doesn't look like a hiker to me."

Dave pushed him roughly to the bed. "You're wearing far too many clothes." He undid the Velcro snaps to Aaron's fly and slid the shorts down his legs.

"Yoo-Hoo! I need more coffee!" Mrs. Halliday's voice trilled from outside their door.

Aaron froze underneath Dave as his husband got on top of him.

"Tell me you locked it," Aaron breathed as Dave moved between Aaron's knees and began licking and kissing his way up Aaron's body.

"Yeah . . ."

"Hello? Anybody home?" She banged harder this time.

"Maybe I should get up and make her some." Aaron started to rise, but Dave grabbed him by the wrists and held them up over Aaron's head, pinning them to the bed.

"I'm willing to risk a bad review," Dave said.

Their gazes locked.

"So am I," Aaron responded as Dave's lips crushed against his. He could feel his husband's massive boner aching for him, imprisoned inside Dave's damp shorts. They could hear their guest stomping away, but Aaron didn't care.

He wanted his husband naked, but Dave was focused on bringing Aaron pleasure. His lips clamped on Aaron's nipples, making them hard. He licked at them, keeping Aaron's arms imprisoned above his head.

Aaron tried to wriggle free but couldn't. Dave licked and kissed his armpits, driving him crazy. At last he moved down the bed, releasing Aaron's wrists. Aaron reached down instantly, pulling off Dave's T-shirt and tossing it to the floor. Dave knelt at the foot of the bed and began sucking Aaron's cock. He stopped for a moment, just holding it in his mouth and released him, toying with it, letting it fall against his tongue, his open mouth sucking him back in greedily.

Once again he released Aaron, opening his legs and cupping his ass cheeks, smiling up at him before diving into his hole. He sucked and licked at Aaron, making him squirm. Aaron humped Dave's face, wanting, needing Dave inside him. He pushed himself away and rolled to his knees, offering Dave his ass.

"Do it. Do it now."

Dave looked dazed as he got to his feet, shucked off his shorts, and joined Aaron once again on the bed. He began nuzzling Aaron's ass as Aaron prepared himself for the pounding he knew he was going to get. He loved fucking Dave every which-way but doggy style was so primal and so deep.

He kept bucking against Dave's tongue, feeling his hole opening up more, relaxing. Dave knew Aaron's body so well. He chose the right moment to take possession of him. Aaron thrilled to Dave's cock pushing at his hole. Dave took his time, rubbing the head against Aaron, slapping it a little.

Aaron moved his hips, rocking from side to side as Dave entered him with a cry. He began to fuck Aaron good and hard, reaching down suddenly, pulling Aaron up by his feet. Aaron collapsed on the bed, his cock trapped beneath his groin as Dave picked up the pace. For a moment Aaron thought his ass would break in two, but he loved it. Loved how much Dave needed him. Aaron fucked the cock in his ass, squeezing, bearing down on it, aware at the exact moment Dave began to come.

Oh, Aaron loved how excited Dave got, the way he gripped Aaron's hips and pumped, harder, faster, reaching to Aaron's belly and grabbing his cock. Aaron moved his ass up, his cock now in Dave's determined grip. He stroked Aaron rapidly until they both came. Aaron became aware of the ocean waves outside, the crashing and soaring sound. As if the sea was matching their own orgasmic swell.

They fell to the bed again, laughing, Dave kissing Aaron's back.

"That was a heart starter," he murmured.

Aaron half turned, to capture his husband's kiss and closed his mouth, savoring the bliss.

As they reluctantly left their hideaway to tend to their guests, Aaron spied the Lokelani roses he'd brought here the day before. That seemed such a long time ago, now. He'd handle his visitors, prepare the new guest bedrooms, and then he'd come back and restore their private quarters, erasing all trace of Troy's handiwork.

Dave's cell phone beeped and he checked the messages. "Hey, the limo's ready. We have to rent a car until we replace the other one, so maybe we can ask Alice to take us to pick up the limo then you and I can drive to the airport for a rental."

"Sounds good." Aaron picked up the roses.

"What are you doing with those?"

"Just something I have to do. Something between me and Troy."

Dave instantly reached for him. "Are you okay?"

"I'm fine, babe. I'll be in the house in a minute."

They exchanged a swift kiss and left the house, Aaron walking to the beach alone. He stared at the blooms in his hand then out to the churning water.

He began to sob. "You know they say there are no roses for a sailor's grave. Well, for you, Troy, there are." He threw them into the crest of a wave, sea foam licking at his feet.

"I wish you'd loved me just a little." He wiped his eyes with the backs of his hands and gazed up at the sky. "But you didn't. Thank you for letting him go in the end. You must have loved him a lot to do that. And this is where you and I say goodbye."

Aaron couldn't bear the idea of a funeral. A grave. He would never claim his twin's ashes. He would ask the state officials to cast them out to sea.

"And just so you know," he said, "when I walk away, I will not look back." He swallowed, the tears flooding his face. "But rest assured, brother, I will love him enough . . . for both of us."

He turned on his heel, headed back to the house, a great weight lifted from his head and heart. Outside the house, Dave beckoned him. Aaron's body responded. He began to run, faster and faster until he could smell, taste, and touch David's skin again.

The End

You may also enjoy the following from eXtasy Books Inc:

Artificial Moonlight
AJ Llewellyn and DJ Manly

Excerpt

When I arrived, I paid the parking fee, secured my bike, and went to locate the others. Chase and Nuts had found beer and were sitting under a tree right at the end of the field.

Chase looked up at me when I approached. "You seen the others?"

"They got cut off. They'll be along. A lot of traffic. Where are the hang arounds?"

Nuts handed me a cold beer. "They've gone to do the registering and shit."

I nodded my thanks and popped the cap. I leaned against the tree and drank down half of it. It felt good to move around. "Any food around here?"

"Want me to go get you some burgers, Diego?" One of the hang arounds asked. They were like trained puppies.

"I'll get something later," I said.

"How's the ribs?" Chase cocked an eyebrow at me.

"Okay, now that I'm not riding. No thanks to you, asshole," I looked at him.

"You need to be in shape for the fight in a few months."

"Yeah," I said. "No worries."

He stood. "Well, one of you guys come with me, the other can wait here and supervise the setting up. I got a meeting."

"I'll stay," I said. "I'm beat. I want a shower, and I want to sleep. Any place for a shower around here?"

"I think you gotta pay." Nuts hooked a thumb. "Careful. Don't get accosted by some pervert." He chuckled and drained his beer can.

I narrowed my eyes. "Fuck you." I looked at Chase. "I thought we weren't doing business this time."

"It's a brief meeting, nothing I can't handle. Just a little connection with a Texas gang I want to secure."

I nodded.

Arnold was coming with the van now. He stopped to speak with Chase and Nuts, drove up to where I was standing, and parked.

"Perfect," I said, going around back. I wanted my stuff.

I opened the door. Dave and Camden, two of the other members, jumped on me and knocked me to the ground, hollering like fiends. I swore and pushed them away.

"Boo," Dave said, poking out his hand.

I took it, and he pulled me to my feet. We laughed.

"Where are the others?" I asked.

"They're going with Chase and Nuts," Camden said. "That Marcel is coming with more of his pals. They'll set shit up."

I climbed in the back of the van and found my bag. I really wanted a shower. "Arnie, where are the showers?" I asked him when I was back on the ground.

"Want me to take you?" he asked as he began to pull out the tents.

"No, you got your hands full. Just point the way."

"You gotta walk all the way down there." He pointed. "I think you got to pay something, or it might be included in the price. Don't know."

I shrugged. "Okay." I slung my duffle bag over my

shoulder and walked down the path. On either side of me, people were settling in with their trailers and tents. Either people nodded at me or turned away when they saw me. That was pretty typical. I struck fear in people's hearts. It was the vest with the shrunken head hanging on a stick and the big, bold letters declaring me a member of the Banni de Louisiane. The patches on the front indicated that I was sergeant in arms. To people in the know, it meant that my job was to kick ass. And my size confirmed I'd have no trouble doing that.

I found the showers. I checked my watch and saw that it was eight o'clock, which explained the throng of kids in a variety of superhero pajamas all brushing their teeth over this trough-like thing with continual water running.

Some of the kids ran into me and squealed. I laughed as they ran off to their respective tents. I walked into the shower room on the men's side. They were free to use. There were ten independent showers stalls with a separate space to leave your stuff while you showered.

I took off my watch, my boots, and my clothes, and laid them carefully on the allotted shelf. I took special care with the vest. I found shampoo and soap in my kit, took a towel out of my bag, then got under the spray. The water wasn't too hot, but it didn't matter. I shampooed my hair, rubbed a hand over my rough jaw, and decided a shave could wait. I'd find a barber somewhere in the next day or two. I checked my ribs and noticed the bruising was almost gone.

I dried off and put on some clean clothes — jeans, my boots, and pulled a navy-blue T-shirt over my head. I rubbed the excess water out of my hair and brushed it out. I felt like a new man.

I picked up my vest and carried it outside, along with my bag. I'd taken two steps when I heard, "Well, hello, handsome. I guess it must be fate."

I couldn't believe my eyes when I saw him standing there. "The car guy? Shit. You gotta be kidding me!"

He laughed and came closer. Now that I had a good look

at him, oh baby, did I like what I saw. His hair was thick and dark brown, and he had blue eyes — beautiful blue eyes — and a generous mouth. He was about six feet tall, nice and slim, with some intriguing tone. He was wearing a red muscle shirt and a pair of jean shorts. Those shorts were tight in all the right places.

"Is that what you call me?" He chuckled. "How cute. The car guy. Name's Colby, actually, but you can just call me 'baby.'"

I shook my head. "Do you know who I am?"

His gaze moved to the vest in my hand. "From the looks of it, you're some big shot with the Banni."

"You could get killed talking to me like that."

"I could die looking into your eyes; that's for sure."

"Well . . ." I cleared my throat, looking around. "That could be arranged."

"The dying or the looking into your eyes part?"

"Both," I told him.

"Woohoo, a macho man, threatening to kill me now. I would wager," He moved closer and placed a hand on my chest. "You'd have a hell of a lot more fun fucking me than killing me."

"Who are you?" I shook my head in wonder and pushed his hand away.

"Told you, my name is — "

"No, no, I mean . . . damn it, boy."

He smiled. "You like my style?"

"If you like the suicidal type, I guess."

He laughed. "You have a sense of humor."

"What are you doing here? Surely you're not sleeping here in this place."

"Why? 'Cause I have a fancy car?"

"Yeah, because you have a fancy car," I mocked.

He laughed again. "If you think I'm a little rich boy, you'd be right. At least, my daddy is."

"Where are you from?"

"The same place you're from, sweetheart. Good, old Louisiana. And you're Cajun."

"How would you know that?"

"I just do. You look it. And although you speak very good English, you sound Cajun. There's a lovely little twang in your voice. You might have a good mix of Creole too . . . Spanish and . . . French, even a little café au lait?"

He was right on. My mother was Creole.

"It's incredibly intoxicating and sexy. In fact, you radiate sex. How bloody tall are you anyway?"

I didn't answer. "You're a little crazy, aren't you?"

"Maybe." He cocked his head. "But I'm the type of guy who knows what he wants when he sees it." He licked his lips, reached over, and grabbed a strand of my hair.

I knocked his hand away.

"You're still wet. I could've come in there and licked you dry."

"Really? How helpful of you."

"I want you. In fact, I want to wrap myself in that long hair of yours. I don't care if you're a biker, a dancer, or you work for the French Foreign Legion. I want what's in those pants. And you know what?" He moved up beside me and seemed to inhale me. "You want me, too. In fact, right now you're thinking about how you'd like to drag me into that shower you just got out of and fuck the hell out of me. You want to pump me until I beg for mercy, and then fuck me all over again."

I was breathless. Damn it. He could read my mind, and believe me, it was rated triple X. "Where are you staying?" I asked him, glancing around.

"I have a hotel room, all to myself." He met my gaze. The meaning was clear. "If you have balls like I think those colors you wear imply, you'll come by later and check out what I have to offer." He pulled a piece of paper and a pen out of his pocket, scribbled something, then pressed the piece of paper in my hand. "Address and room. It's a suite, really. It's got a hot tub."

I cleared my throat. "Don't hold your breath."

"I have some friends waiting for me. I promised to join them for a bonfire. I'll be at the hotel around midnight. I'll wait up." He met my gaze again. "Unless you're scared."

"Scared?" I raised my eyebrow. "Scared of what? You?"

He smiled. "You did almost get yourself killed, racing away from me earlier."

I scowled.

He laughed again. "Gotcha, beautiful."

"You like to play dangerous games, don't you?"

"Yes," he said. "I do. And you are the most dangerous and delicious game I've ever played. Jesus, you make my head spin."

"You could end up hurting."

"I'll take my chances. That's part of the thrill, isn't it? Now, if you were as willing to push the envelope as I am, you'd kiss me right now."

I took a step. I almost grabbed him and pulled him into the bushes, but then I saw Marcel heading toward me. "Get lost," I told him, and I crumpled up the paper and pushed it into my pocket.

"On one condition," he said. "Tell me your name."

"Diego," I grunted. "Now go."

He walked off in the other direction just as Marcel came up and took my bag. "How was the shower?"

"Fine," I said. I'd broken out in a damn sweat.

"We're set up. You hanging around or going somewhere?"

I took a breath. I glanced at the bonfire a few feet away. I could see the guy sitting there, talking and laughing with his friends. I knew his gaze was on me as I walked by with Marcel. I didn't look in his direction. "I'm going to get some sleep," I told him. "I'm beat."

My tent was ready when I got back. I said a few words to the guys, then crawled into the sleeping bag inside my tent. I knew I wasn't going to be able to sleep, not only because the other guys were talking loudly, but also because I couldn't stop thinking about that insane Colby guy. He was crazy gorgeous, and he wanted me, and that was wildly exciting. I knew I could get up and leave at any time, find my way to his hotel. I had only to put my jeans back on, reach in, and pull out the crumpled piece of paper I'd shoved into my pocket. I'd ride downtown, have a drink at one of the bars, and then if I still felt like it, I could drop by his room. Maybe I'd just fuck him and leave. What was the harm in that? He'd invited me, hadn't he? He was some kind of crazy.

What the hell.

About the Authors

A.J. Llewellyn is the author of almost three hundred published gay romance novels. A.J. lives in California, but dreams of living in Hawaii. Frequent trips to all the islands, bags of Kona coffee in the fridge and a healthy collection of Hawaiian records keep A.J. refueled.

A.J's passion for the islands led to writing a play about the last ruling monarch of Hawaii, Queen Lili'uokalani. A.J. has written a non-erotic novel about the overthrow of her kingdom written in diary form from her maid's point of view.

A.J. never lacks inspiration for male/male erotic romances and has to prise fingers from the computer keyboard to pursue other passions: collecting books on Hawaiiana, surfing and spending time with family, friends and animal companions.

D.J. Manly: I write not only for my own pleasure but for the pleasure of my readers. I can't remember a time in my life when I haven't written and told stories. When I'm not writing, I'm dreaming about writing, doing something wild and adventurous, or trying to make the world a better and more open-minded place to live in. I adore beautiful men, and I know I'm not alone in this! Eroticism between consenting adults, in all its many forms, is the icing on the cake of life!

D.J. has published well over two hundred novels/novellas and is a well-seasoned writer.

www.ingramcontent.com/pod-product-compliance
Lightning Source LLC
Chambersburg PA
CBHW060618130626
46555CB00002B/555